Home and Away Games

By Greg Cielec

My Cleveland Story (1998)

Home and Away Games

A novella

By Greg Cielec

Also includes excerpts from the novels
My Cleveland Story and
A Poem on a Bar Room Wall

Pink Flamingo Press and Creative Endeavors
Cleveland, Ohio
2006

Home and Away Games
First Edition
Copyrighted 2006 by Greg Cielec
Copyrighted 2006 by Pink Flamingo Press and Creative Endeavors
ISBN 0-9665724-1-6

"The Big Game" is an excerpt from the novel *My Cleveland Story*,
copyrighted 1998 by Pink Flamingo Press and Greg Cielec

"All Laughs and No Tears" is an excerpt from the upcoming novel *A Poem on a
Bar Room Wall*. Copyrighted 2006 by Greg Cielec

Lyrics from "Long Time Loving You" by John Schwab, copyrighted 1980 by
John Schwab and McGuffey Lane Music

Cover Artwork and Design by Kristi Quisenberry
Interior Design by Greg Cielec and Dave Hostetler

The author would personally like to thank Dave Hostetler,
Polly Dierkens, Nikki Lee, Brenda Alderson, and Kristi Quisenberry
for their help on this project.

Printed in the United States of America
Pink Flamingo Press and Creative Endeavors
1528 Botany Avenue
Cleveland, Ohio 44109

A note from the author:

The book that you hold in your hands contains a novella, as well as excerpts reworked as short stories from two novels.

The novella "Home and Away Games" started out as an attempt to write a screenplay. I was having trouble with the format, but really liked the story. My original plan was to write the story out first as a short story, then as a screenplay. I thought it would end up being ten to twelve pages, but it obviously ended up being a bit longer.

"The Big Game" is an excerpt from my first novel, *My Cleveland Story*, which came out in time for the holidays in 1998 and is still with us today. Although it did not make a major national splash on the literary world, it did go through several printings and is still hanging in there, years later. Not a week has gone by since it was published when I haven't gotten a letter, email, or phone call from someone who tells me they just read it and wants to talk about it.

"All Laughs and No Tears" is from my next novel, *A Poem on a Bar RoomWall*, which is in progress. I wish I could give you a publication date, but I can't. Hopefully it will be soon. You can periodically check my website (www.gregcielec.com) for updates and other excerpts.

This book is dedicated to Joe and Marlene,
who kept the home and away games under control
while raising four teenagers back in the fabulous seventies.

Home and Away Games

"I can't blame you for not believin',
In a man you only see on a phone."
from "Long Time Loving You" by John Schwab

"Without a family, man, alone in the world, trembles with the cold."
Andre Maurois

"Every coach's wife is a single mom."
Shiela Priefer

Prologue
Nine Months Earlier

Gina knew she would never forget the taste of both of those boys in her mouth. And how one held her down, and the other forced his way into her. How stupid can I be? *she kept saying to herself.* And what am I going to do when Mom finds out? I know damn well what she's going to.

She sat in the front seat of the car, staring out the window, tears flowing down her raw face, bouncing back and forth between drunkenness and sobriety. She tried to hold onto the straight and narrow, but the alcohol and pills were still pulling her head in different directions. How could've I been so damn stupid?

When the car pulled up in front of her house, she got out without turning back. She opened the front door, ignored the voices from the kitchen, ran up the steps, went into her bedroom, and slammed the door behind her. How could I be so damn stupid?

Crying spasms and hiccups came and went as she lay across her bed. She continued drifting between drunkenness and sobriety, as her bed, as well as everything in the room, spun around and around.

Amongst the chaos inside of her head floated the afternoon's events, along with snapshots of her mother and her brother and sister, and even her father. Oh my God, Dad, what's he going to do when he finds out? How can I be so damn stupid?

7

Craig Collier and Emily Johnson sat at the kitchen table, drinking coffee, and making small talk over events from school.

"Yeah, Charlie put Scott into the game and he made his first two baskets. Do you believe that, in a varsity game?" Craig said.

"Well, thank God it happened. That boy needed a shot in the arm. He really has very little self confidence."

The door opened, and Emily knew it was Gina. "Hi, Honey, how was your day? Did you get a lot done?"

Neither Emily or Craig heard Gina reply, just her feet up the steps and her bedroom door slamming.

They both looked at each other with a touch of concern, but got back to their conversation about the first varsity basketball game of the season. But as Emily listened to Craig, her mind kept wandering to her daughter upstairs. After she got up and filled both of their coffee cups, Emily turned to Craig and said, "Excuse me for a second; I know she hasn't been herself at times lately, but that's just not like her not to say hi to us when she comes home."

Craig stayed downstairs sipping his coffee, knowing that Emily was concerned about the time Gina was spending with her new friends.

Suddenly, the pleasant Sunday afternoon was shattered by Emily's near scream from the top of the stairs: "Craig, call 9-1-1 for an ambulance, then get up here as fast as you can."

Chapter One
Sunday

It was a chilly, late autumn Sunday afternoon, almost evening. You knew it was cold by the steam in the breath of the boys in the backyard playing basketball. The game was spirited, despite all of the boys being bundled up in their letter jackets over layers of sweatshirts.

Inside a group of girls sat around the kitchen table, doing their homework and gossiping about school. The table was covered with open textbooks and notebooks, and calculators were being passed around.

Emily Johnson opened the back door and yelled to the boys, "Finish your game, fellas. The pizza will be here soon." This was the world Emily Johnson presided over, and that Sunday everything seemed to be going okay. An attractive woman in her late forties, Emily was mom to one of the boys playing basketball and one of the girls sitting at the table. She also knew most of the other kids from being their English teacher at the high school at one time or another.

For Emily the school year had been going fine, so far. Emily still felt a sense of impending disaster, however. She only had to look back to last year to realize how quickly things could change.

Emily grabbed the coupon taped to the refrigerator door and went into the living room to wait for the pizza man and to check on her third child, ten-year-old Jill, who was sitting by herself doing her own homework.

"How you doing, Beaner?" Emily said as she sat on the couch and ran her fingers through her daughter's hair.

Emily glanced up at the football game on the television. It was the late game from the West Coast and the Raiders were beating the Chargers badly. The bright sun shining on the field, and all the fans in T-shirts and shorts, made the game feel as if it was light years away.

The audio on the television was turned down, but Emily could still hear the announcers comment more than once that a Chargers' loss could put the head coach's job in jeopardy.

"Everything that could go wrong with a team has happened to the Chargers. Injuries, weak drafts, contract holdouts…" The head coach of the Chargers was Sonny Johnson, Emily's ex-husband, and the father of her three children.

Emily watched the game for several minutes as things went from bad to worse. Another Charger turnover gave the Raiders the ball inside the ten; three plays later they scored another touchdown. "There is nothing Sonny Johnson can do as his lifeless team gives up yet another score…"

Back in Ohio, the pizza arrived and everyone huddled around the counter in the kitchen. Emily watched with a casual eye as the two cliques of schoolmates intermingled with each other. They were miles apart last year, but seemed to be spending a fair amount of time together so far this school year, much of it at the Johnson house. The girls, all seniors and some of them cheerleaders, had spent the last two years hanging around a crowd of guys now out of school. The boys, all juniors, were enjoying their first year as varsity jocks. Last year they had been lowly sophomore JVs, slightly above the freshmen on the school's social scale.

Emily knew it was Gina who brought the two cliques together. She had found new appreciation of her friendship with her cheerleading friends because of the support they had given her last year. She also enjoyed playing the role of big sister, not just to her brother Brandon, but to his buddies, setting them up with Homecoming dates, helping them with homework, and decorating their lockers before games.

Jill moved amongst the teenagers unnoticed, definitely carrying a chip on her shoulder because of the attention her older brother, the football player, and her older sister, the cheerleader, seem to garnish this time of year.

Down the street and around the corner from Emily's house, Craig Collier sat with several of his coaching assistants, also eating pizza and watching the Chargers game. Craig, too, had a history with Sonny Johnson, and the Chargers' poor performance bothered him more than he thought it would. *How could those guys quit on him?* he kept saying to himself. The Raiders kept pouring it on the Chargers, and the announcers would not drop the idea that this could be Sonny's last game as a head coach.

"What would he do if he got fired?" someone asked Craig.

"I don't know. He's never been fired before."

"Well, it looks like it's going to happen."

"Hey," someone else said. "Do you think he'd end up here this week? Maybe see our game on Friday?"

Craig contemplated the situation for a moment. "He might end up here. I just hope it's not this week. We have enough to deal with already."

Greg Cielec

Chapter Two
Monday

The next day at school, Brandon Johnson and his buddies settled down for lunch at their usual table in the school's cafeteria. The table in the far corner of the lunchroom was an ideal location for the boys for several reasons: its proximity to the lunch line; the view of every girl in the cafeteria; and the view of the TV mounted in the wall that was tuned to SportsCenter during lunch periods. The boys settled into their usual conversations about what Missy McMichael wore to school that day, how hard their math test was, and what homework was checked and not checked in their morning classes. They would occasionally glance up at the TV, so as not to miss any exciting highlights or news about their favorite teams or players.

Brandon was yacking away about how stupid math class was in the first place, when in mid sentence he stopped. All of his attention turned to the TV set, because filling the screen was the face of his father. Brandon could immediately tell, by the look on his father's face, that it wasn't good news.

"I know some people would look for excuses," Sonny Johnson was saying, as he peered out over the podium into the crowd of reporters. "I accept full responsibility. It would be easier to stand up here and put the blame on contract

12

holdouts, weak draft picks, and some serious injuries to some key players. But I won't do that…"

The screen then switched back to the sports anchor who said: "Johnson was in his fifth season in San Diego after some very successful seasons as a college coach. He finishes with a 42-32 career record, not bad when you consider what he had to work with…and in other news around the league…"

All faces turned to Brandon, who didn't know what to say. He finally got up and said, "I think I better go tell my mom. I'm sure she'll want to know."

Monday dinner has always been very important to Emily Johnson. It was the only night of the whole week that her entire family ate together. Brandon and Gina came home right after football and cheerleading practices, and Jill did not have Brownies or gymnastics. Also usually along to mooch a free meal were Rob Steele and Craig.

"This is the story," Emily said as she put the plate of pot roast on the table and took her seat.

Everyone kept on with their conversations, ignoring her. Emily paused, cleared her throat, and in her best teacher voice said, "Excuse me." By that tone everyone knew she meant business and quieted down.

"Your father left a message on our voice mail. He's coming to visit tomorrow." The news was met with less enthusiasm than one would expect, except from Jill, who had a smile stretched across her cute little face. Everyone except for Jill and Rob Steele had an immediate opinion.

"Where's he going to stay?" Brandon asked.

"Mom, I hope I don't sound negative," Gina said. "I mean, it will be really great to see him. But aren't there some things he should know about?"

"Sounds like it's too late for that," said Brandon, obviously referring to his older sister.

"Hey, young man, you've had a few moments yourself recently, haven't you?" Emily said.

"Yeah," said Gina. "How about getting busted for drinking at the winter formal?"

"And what about your car accident?" asked Emily. "That was a real pleasant moment for everyone involved."

"And what about when I had to bust you guys for chewing tobacco in my class? That was really great, having three of my own players suspended from school," added Craig.

Brandon changed the subject. "Couldn't Dad wait at least one more week before coming?"

Craig nodded his head in agreement with Brandon.

Suddenly everyone started to speak at once, but no one was saying directly what he or she was thinking. Brandon said he hoped he would not be too nervous for his game Friday, but he was remembering what Sonny was like as a Little League parent. Gina voiced her concern about it being such a busy week, that no one would have much time for their dad, but was thinking about who was going to break the news to him about her experience last spring. Craig wondered aloud what Sonny would do while everyone was at school or practice, knowing all along he'd just be busy looking over everyone's shoulders, especially Craig's, being a pain. Emily said she would have to have him over for dinner. Rob Steele sat there, slight smirk on his face, just enjoying another free meal. When he finished he got up and left unnoticed, as voices kept rising to be heard.

The conversation around the table kept going on around Jill, who sat very quietly playing with her mashed potatoes, the ear-to-ear smile still on her face. Suddenly she stopped everyone in their tracks with a dead-on imitation of her mother. First she cleared her throat, and then in her mom's best teaching voice, said firmly, "Excuse me!"

Everyone turned toward the ten-year-old with shocked looks on their faces.

"I know why Daddy's coming," she said.

Emily, in her best mother voice, said, "Oh, Beaner, honey, don't worry about your dad, he'll get another..."

Oblivious to what her mother was saying, Jill blurted out, "Daddy's coming to take me to the dance on Wednesday."

"Dance? What dance?" Emily asked.

"The father and daughter dance. The father and daughter dance at school is this Wednesday and I sent Daddy a letter all about it and asked him to go with me," she said.

Everyone at the table just stared at Jill for a moment or two, and then burst into hearty laughs that broke the tension in the room.

As she lay in bed later that evening, Emily rolled around and around, unable to sleep. *Why this week?* she kept asking herself. Sonny had every right to be near the kids, and Emily wanted him to be a part of their lives, *but why now?*

This was going to be the coming-out week for Emily and her new significant other, Fred Graham. They were going to sit with each other at Friday's game, and then attend the coach's party afterward together. It would be their first appearance together in front of many of her friends and co-workers.

And what about Sonny? Even though she never talked to anyone about her marriage to Sonny, and despite all that had happened, she never really got him completely out of her system after all of these years. That's how much she had loved him at one time. Her current interest in Fred Graham was her first attempt at a relationship in years, probably since they moved back to Ohio. It had literally been years since she had last seen Sonny. It had also been at least that many years since she was around someone that she was really attracted to; now she would be around two of them at the same time.

In the bedroom next to Emily's, Gina could not sleep either. Different thoughts kept floating through her head: beautiful Carolina spring days, walking through the field behind their old farm house, hand-in-hand with her father; the ugly arguments between her mother and father about moving to California; and, of course, bits and pieces of her Sunday from hell.

In her bedroom down the hall from her mother and sister, Jill couldn't fall asleep either. She was too excited about going shopping Tuesday after school with her mom for a dress for Wednesday's dance. *How jealous will Brandon and Gina be when I walk down the steps in a new dress and Daddy will be waiting for me*, she kept saying to herself.

In his room next to Jill's, Brandon had no trouble falling asleep. Sure, he was a little apprehensive about his father showing up this week, but he'd worry about that tomorrow. Brandon fell asleep thinking about the same things he thought about every night: Missy McMichael's beautiful brown hair falling onto her shoulders; Missy McMichael's mysterious deep brown eyes; Missy McMichael's sexy, luscious lips; and Missy McMichael's voluptuous breasts bouncing around inside of her cheerleading sweater.

Down the street and around the corner, Craig went to bed that night also unable to fall asleep, with Friday's game, and Sonny Johnson, on his mind.

Craig Collier and Sonny Johnson first crossed paths when Craig was one of Sonny's players at a small Division III football school in Ohio. They had a couple of good years together, including two league championships and a play-off appearance. Both would always say they had a great group of guys on the team, and Craig would say all the players loved Sonny and all the other coaches.

As much as the guys on the team loved Sonny, they were all in love with Emily Johnson. She was more than just the coach's wife; she was their ideal of the woman they all hoped to marry someday. She was the sexy, slightly older woman they all fell over. She was blonde and shapely and had mesmerizing blue eyes that you couldn't stop staring at. Each year she and Sonny would have the team over to their house for a cookout the night before summer practices started, and all the players would talk afterwards about how each wanted to find a woman like her.

After Craig's sophomore year, Sonny left to be an assistant at one of the Mid-American Conference schools, and three years later he was head coach and Craig was one of his graduate assistants. They would become MAC champions, win the Vegas Bowl, and be well on their way to the big time. Soon Sonny was offered the head job at one of the Atlantic Coast Conference schools, and Craig tagged along as a graduate assistant there also.

By that time Sonny and Emily had three small children.

The move to Carolina did not go smoothly for Emily and the kids. It was the third time in five years Gina and Brandon were switching schools and leaving behind yet another group of friends. And this one was different because the move was far. The earlier moves were all within Ohio, and they never were that far away from Emily's family. It was never more than a drive down the freeway to visit grandparents or attend a cousin's birthday party. All that changed with the move to Carolina.

Emily found a nice farmhouse about twenty minutes from campus, but Sonny kept even longer hours at school. If recruiting was an eighteen-hour-a-day job before, it was 24/7 in the big time. Sonny slept in his office two or three times a week.

Emily soon started to despise being "Mrs. Sonny Johnson, the Coach's wife." She soon realized that whenever she was invited to something, or when someone went out of their way to be nice to her, it was under that pretense, and that she was obliged to sit and smile and play the role.

During her first two stints as the head coach's wife, Emily was able to stay out of the limelight. But in the big time, as she would years later tell Craig, "They thought they owned me." Her social responsibilities were more demanding than the university president's wife, with luncheons, charity events, and fundraisers. It never ended, and Emily soon hated it. She just wanted to be a stay-at-home mom, and one day, when the kids got a little older, maybe return to the classroom as a teacher.

But Emily and the kids adjusted. Sonny's first two years at Carolina were very successful, going 6-5 and then 9-2 and playing in the Sugar Bowl. Sonny and his staff really turned the team around, recruiting went great, and the future looked very bright.

Most of the same coaches came over with Sonny to Carolina, and they all enjoyed the big time. They were all like Sonny, and buried themselves in their jobs. In season they were at the office for six a.m. meetings, and rarely left before eight at night. Even during the off-season, the hours changed little.

The coaches all got to the point, in that mentality that is big time coaching, that if you didn't put in very long hours then you didn't want to win. So what did they start to do all day, especially in the off-season? They broke down game films that already had been broken down four times; they went to meetings to discuss practice plans for practices six months in the future; and they watched video of not only next year's recruits, but the year after that as well.

And while the coaches were doing all of that, it was their families who suffered. The wives were a bunch of classy ladies who were good moms with beautiful kids. But things started to unravel, and the coaches didn't realize it until it was too late. One wife had an affair with a neighbor, another asked for a divorce and moved back to Ohio. Others accepted the situation as a fact of life, and adjusted. The women had all only been married to coaches; and they really didn't know any different.

That's what Emily did. She knew that Sonny's dream was to be a head coach at a big time college, and she was willing to build their lives around that. It might not be an ideal situation, but it would be good enough.

17

From DIII to the MAC to the ACC, Craig got to know Emily and the other wives pretty well, and thought the world of all of them. The coach's wives and their children were their own little support system, and he would occasionally float in and out of it. Craig especially liked many of the kids, because he had known most of them from birth, and he enjoyed seeing them grow up.

And just when Emily felt things were getting a little better, just when the kids finally felt somewhat adjusted and had started the year in the same school for three years in a row, and everyone started to think that this wasn't a bad place to spend the next ten years of their lives, the pros called.

At first Sonny said no; he had everything he ever wanted. His salary was bumped up every year, the team was a regular in the Top 25, and two straight bowl appearances made the boosters and alumni relatively happy.

But the pros would not take no for an answer, raising the ante with each phone call. Finally, when the pot on the table got into the millions, Sonny couldn't say no. And Emily was upset.

"Honey, it's just too much money to say no to," he said.

"Sonny, we're making more money now then we ever dreamed of. What do we need more for? This was your dream. You have what you always said you wanted."

But ego and ambition came before family life, and Sonny took the San Diego job and headed west immediately. Emily remained behind with the kids, refusing to pull them out of school before the year was out.

When the school year ended and Emily did pull the kids out of school, it wasn't for the move to San Diego. It was back to Ohio, to the town Emily grew up in, where she started teaching at the high school she once attended.

Craig had left Carolina a year earlier, after their Sugar Bowl year. He had finally finished his master's, and Sonny just assumed he would stay on as a full-time assistant. And although he loved football and enjoyed coaching, Craig was really burnt out on it. In his three years in DI Craig had watched too much game film, kissed too many recruits' asses, and helped too many irresponsible players write term papers and get out of trouble. It was time for a change, and maybe Craig needed some time away from Sonny too.

Craig had heard about Emily and the kids moving to Ohio secondhand through phone calls and letters from mutual friends. He spent two years down in

Florida teaching and coaching high school, pretty much the only place you could really get a teaching job at the time. The school was too big and overcrowded, the weather was too hot most of the time, but Craig did find out something very important about himself: that he liked teaching and it gave him a feeling of self worth. The guys he taught and coached with couldn't believe he walked away from a spot on Sonny Johnson's coaching staff to teach high school social studies. But the two years Craig spent in south Florida were good years, and he might still be there if he hadn't gotten a call from Emily.

Craig had been surprised as anyone when Emily and the kids moved back to Ohio, and not to San Diego. He had seen Sonny drifting from his family and knew Emily wasn't happy, but he never expected them to split. He just assumed, like almost everyone else, that Emily and the kids would follow Sonny out west. In fact, he never accepted it as a fact until Emily called one night and asked him if he would be interested in the head football job at the school where she was teaching. It was small town Ohio, but not too far from where Craig had grown up and from where he had gone to college. He arranged for a Friday off, got a cheap flight from Orlando to Columbus, rented a car, had an interview, and the next thing he knew, took the job.

When he moved back to Ohio, Craig saw that Emily and her kids seemed to be living a good life without Sonny. Emily was teaching high school English and really enjoying it. She was a natural teacher and could really connect with the students. Gina and Brandon were now in middle school, and were into all that good stuff like sports and cheerleading and dances and parties. They seemed more at home in Ohio, and liked living in a town with grandparents and cousins nearby. Jill was in grade school, and loved being around her peers instead of just being somebody's little sister. Emily never spoke of her marriage to Sonny to anyone again, and she let everyone know that it was behind her.

The first few years back in Ohio, Sonny didn't seem to be that far away. The kids all had an abundance of Chargers hats, shirts, and sweaters to wear to school, and Chargers team posters covered the kids' bedroom walls. They would frequently talk to Sonny on the phone, and in the off-season he would sometimes come and spend a day or two. If San Diego had a game in Cleveland, Cincinnati or Detroit, Craig would drive the kids and some of their friends to see it. And, of course, the kids would go out to California to spend a few weeks with Sonny each summer during training camp.

As the kids got older, they started to drift away from their father. Their lives just became too busy, and there wasn't as much time as before for long distance phone calls or letter writing. Even their summer trips to California got shortened, so as to not conflict with baseball games and cheerleading camps. Sonny no longer would pop in unannounced, and it got to the point that both Craig and Emily went almost three years without seeing him.

Emily became Craig's teaching mentor at school, and they became quite close friends. They shared a good deal of each other's past; however, they never discussed her marriage to Sonny, or the end of it. Emily never volunteered any information, and Craig never asked.

After going nearly two years without seeing her, there was one change Craig did notice in Emily. She was still a very attractive woman, and she was aging gracefully, but her eyes showed that she had gone through a change. They were still a beautiful vivid blue, but they now had a touch of sadness to them.

Chapter Three
Tuesday

During lunch on Tuesday, Brandon and his locker partner and best friend, Johnny Adams, went to Craig's room to discuss the situation.

Brandon had a bad sophomore year of high school, and it took a toll on Emily. Because she was a member of the school's faculty, and had come from one of the older and more established families in town, it seemed like she was the one always caught in the middle, hearing about it from all directions.

Brandon had been a model citizen so far his junior year, owed mostly to the fact that he and his buddies were a year older, and a year wiser. After the last incident, getting suspended for the beer at the dance, he started to realize how much stress each of these incidents had put on his mom. She didn't say a thing when she came to pick him up that night, but the look on her face and the hurt in her eyes got the message across to him.

After the beer incident, Craig got Brandon and his buddies into the coach's office, closed the door, and yelled at them for fifteen minutes. He told them they were stupid for doing it in the first place, and stupid for getting caught. He told them they were stupid for letting down their parents, and stupid for letting down their teammates and coaches.

Sometimes yelling is all that a coach can do.

"I just don't know why you're so uptight about your old man showing up," Johnny said.

"You don't understand, it's not that I don't want him around, it's just that we're not ready for it," Brandon was saying as the three of them sat in Craig's classroom.

"All I know is that I haven't seen my old man in eight years, and I'm still mad at him, but I'd be thrilled if he came and saw our game Friday night," said Johnny.

"I wish that's when he showed up, just for the game Friday, but the rest of the time I don't know. Everything is a vacation as far as my dad goes. We go out there to visit each summer and all we do is fun stuff. Disneyland, the beach, Padres games, and then a week of training camp."

"What's wrong with that?" Craig interjected.

"Nothing, for three weeks a year. But even for that time, it's not like he's really a parent."

Johnny and Craig responded with blank stares.

"Like one time we were out there and Gina got stung by a bee at the zoo and had some sort of allergic reaction. My dad freaked! You know what he did? He took her to the emergency room and then called my grandmother in Pennsylvania and flew her out there to take care of her. Since then, every time we have gone to California my grandmother has been there."

"The man is a great guy, but he knows nothing about being a real parent. I mean, it's cool to have a dad who coaches in the pros, and I get to go to training camp every year and sometimes one of his games, that's really cool. But the man has had four children and still doesn't know how to change a diaper."

"Man, even I know how to change one of those suckers," Johnny laughed.

"He doesn't have a clue about what's going on in our lives back here. He doesn't know anything about what happened to Gina, he doesn't know anything about the day-to-day life of any of us. He doesn't even know how we are doing in school."

"How's he not going to find out about Gina?"

"I think my mom is just going to come out and tell him. Plus, do you remember the last time he saw one of our games?"

Craig and Johnny didn't know what he was talking about.

"Pony League Baseball tournament? About four years ago, in Toledo?"

"Oh, man, I remember," Johnny said. "Did he call that umpire a 'god damn stupid idiot,' or 'a stupid god damn idiot?'"

"Very funny. I can see it now: the world's worst Little League dad seeing his son play high school football for the first time. It definitely sounds like a disaster waiting to happen."

"Hey, does he know about your mom's new squeeze?" John asked.

"Dude, how did you know about that?" Brandon responded, very surprised.

"This is a small town," Johnny replied. "Everyone knows about stuff like that."

"And does he know about you and Missy McMichael?" Craig threw in to be funny.

"Yeah, that you've been in love with her since seventh grade, but have been afraid to talk to her since eighth," kidded Johnny.

"Very funny. Where does the part come where Trey Horton rips my arms out of my shoulder sockets?" Brandon said.

"I'm telling you, it's over between the two of them. She's *never* not had a boyfriend until now. Here's your chance," Craig said.

"As long as you're afraid to talk to her you have two chances," said Johnny. "Little and none."

All three of them burst into laughter.

It had been a dramatic school year so far for Missy McMichael. Last year she had been the sweetheart of the junior class and dated Trey Horton, last year's football captain who had received a full ride to the University of Toledo. Early in the fall, Missy had played the part of the senior girl with the boyfriend away at college. She wore a UT sweatshirt or sweater to school every day, and e-mailed Trey at least three times daily. But all that changed the Sunday before Homecoming, when Missy, Gina and a few other friends drove up to UT to pay Trey a surprise visit. The big surprise came when they walked in on Trey in bed with a Pi Phi, and Trey mumbling, "Maybe it's time we finished this." She was crushed. And what was worse was that all this happened in front of her friends, and that meant everyone at school knew by Monday lunch.

Missy had sworn off boys for the rest of the fall. She didn't attend the Homecoming dance, even after being the junior attendant the year before. Visions of Trey in bed with that other girl still haunted her. In her sheltered life, this was the first time she had something happen to her that wasn't according to plan, and she didn't handle it well.

If Brandon was ever going to have a chance with her, it was now. More than a few people thought they'd make a nice couple.

Tuesday afternoon Sonny Johnson walked into the Armstrong Central coaching office just like he had walked into every other coaching office for the last twenty years: like he owned the place. Craig and his assistants were busy changing into their practice garb and going over the day's practice plan, when they were interrupted by the former Associated Press College and AFC Coach of the Year saying, "What a dump. Who's head coach around here? Doesn't anyone clean up around here?"

Without missing a beat Craig responded, "Your housekeeping budget in San Diego was bigger than our whole budget put together." Craig got out of his seat and shook the hand of his former mentor. "It's good to see you, Sonny." Although it had been a few years since they had seen each other, and their working relationship ended on not-so-good terms years ago, you could tell that they were genuinely happy to see one another.

The other coaches in the room were in awe. Although they had been teaching and coaching his children for years, this was the first time any of them had ever met Sonny Johnson. To meet a coach from the big time was something that didn't happen too often.

Craig introduced all of his assistants to Sonny, and then got everyone back on task. "We're all set then? Usual time for individual, thirty minutes team O, twenty minutes team D. Then we'll go on the field and do kickoff and kick return. Any problems?"

"Martinez and Rhinehart are in detention, so maybe we'd like to go defense first," said one assistant.

"You're right. Sounds good to me." And the coaches, along with Sonny, walked out to the field.

Brandon was up front near the captains for stretching and plyometrics. He turned around when he heard Craig call his name from across the field.

"Brandon, come over here. There's someone here to see you."

Brandon turned around and started to jog and he looked up and knew right away that it was his dad standing with the other coaches. The hair, the stocky build, his great smile. Brandon broke out in a smile of his own, as he was truly happy and excited to see him. Brandon picked up the pace and then stopped in front of the coaches.

"Hi Dad, it's great to see you," he said, putting his hand out for the awkward handshake that always began encounters with his father.

"Hi, Son. It's great to see you," Sonny replied. Craig silently signaled the other coaches to go meet the kids, and to leave Sonny and Brandon alone.

Brandon talked first: "I'm really sorry about what happened in San Diego, I mean…"

"Aw, don't worry about. It's all part of the game," Sonny replied. "Speaking of games, I hear you guys have a big one."

"Yeah we do…"

"So you go on to practice. We'll talk later," Sonny said. He watched his son turn around and jog over to the team.

After a few minutes surveying the field, Sonny came over and asked Craig, "Who's number 87? Looks like he has some tools."

"Rob Steele, tight end," Craig said. "Not only the tools, he is the toughest kid I've ever been around."

"He's a senior?"

"Yeah."

"Who's looking at him?"

"No one. His grades are crap. But the last year or so he's rallied, and he still might make it. He'll be a find for someone."

"What kind of family?"

"There isn't any."

"What?"

"The kid lives on his own. Mom's dead. Dad's in jail, we think. I'll tell you about him later."

Halfway through practice Craig knew he had two major problems for this week's game against Upper Olentangy. The first was at center. Ricky Gustafson, the starting center, had broken his hand in the last game and was unable to play center this week. His hand was too swollen, and he couldn't grip the ball to snap it. Gus had played center for three years, and his only backup was Tommy Wysocki, a skinny sophomore who was at least a year away from being a varsity player. However, the team needed a center for this Friday and Wysocki was the only kid on the team who could snap the ball and step at the same time. Hitting anyone after that was another story.

The second problem was Sonny. If Craig didn't find something for him to do he was going to drive the whole team, the coaches included, crazy. While doing their individual position drills, Sonny interrupted each group, showing everyone a better way to do it. The fact that he was right each time was beside the point. If Craig let him keep going, by Friday he'd be calling both the offense and defense.

During a water break before team up Craig got next to Sonny, made some small talk, and then told him about the situation at center. "We need someone to work with Wysocki, keep an eye on him. He's never played in a varsity game yet." Sonny just nodded his head.

Imagine the look on Tommy Wysocki's face when the former NCAA and AFC Coach of the Year started to tutor him after every play from that moment on. And nothing was right. Even though Sonny wasn't totally familiar with the offense, he knew when a step was wrong, when Wysocki was unsure of what to do, when Wysocki let the other guy hit him before he hit him first.

Sonny even stayed out on the field with Wysocki for fifteen minutes after practice to work on his steps and alignment.

When Sonny finally made it back into the coach's office, he had a look of concern on his face. "Don't you think you should put kids at positions where they can physically play?"

All the coaches burst into laughter. "Sonny," Craig said, "We only have 250 boys in the school. We have the fifty best, give or take a couple, playing football. We can't claim a center off waivers or trade for one. We have to do with what we got."

Sonny saw the logic in what was said. "Now don't you worry, we'll get him straightened out by Friday. Oh, and give me some film on these guys you're playing Friday, and on you guys. I'll look at it tonight to get an idea of what you're trying to do. And one last thing. What color uniforms will Friday's opponent be wearing?"

"Green."

"Green like Baylor, or green like Tulane?"

"Like Baylor. Why?"

"If Wysocki is going to get the job done this Friday it's going to take a little magic."

Craig reached over to the shelf and grabbed several videotapes and handed them to him. Just then Brandon and Rob Steele appeared at the doorway.

"Ready?" Brandon asked.

"Are you?" Craig said to Sonny.

"For what?"

"Dinner. My treat."

Some of the old timers still called it Hamburger Inn, but to most everyone it was simply The Diner. Every so often a new place would open out by the freeway and take away business, but a week or two later everyone would be back. It was one of the true social centers of the town, and from the moment it opened for breakfast at five in the morning, until it closed at nine after the dinner rush, the place was never not crowded. And, needless to say, every important topic was up for discussion amongst the regulars.

Being the head football coach in a small Ohio town, Craig was known to everyone. When he walked in with Sonny, it caused quite a scene. Everyone in the place, from the regulars to the kitchen help, found an excuse to come over to talk to Craig and meet Sonny.

By the time their meals came the excitement had died down. They were finally left alone. All the attention Sonny had received broke the ice, and he and Craig got caught up on old friends, former players, and fellow coaches. Rob Steele and Brandon wolfed down their meals, and then headed back to the kitchen to clean a day's worth of pots and pans.

Craig could tell something had started to bother Sonny, probably the disappointment he felt in seeing his one time protégé now coaching high school in a small railroad town in Ohio. Sonny, at one time, had big plans for Craig; he always said Craig had so much potential.

When talk came back around to football and the time they had spent together, Sonny asked, "Don't you miss it?"

"Miss what? Bailing Freddie Williams out of jail after a bar fight? Writing term papers for Tommy Laxton? Working eighteen hours a day for peanuts because if you don't walk around dead tired all the time people will think you aren't dedicated?"

"What about the money? You'd been making a lot more money with me than you do as a high school teacher."

"Sonny, if it was about money I'd be working on Wall Street."

"But what about everything else? The winning…the traditions?"

"We won for the same reason we win on this level: better players. You might think it was because we watched all that film and were super prepared and we were the smarter coaches, but 95% of the time it's the team with the best players, no matter who is coaching. Look what happened to you in San Diego. When you had the players, you went to the Super Bowl. But after a couple of lousy drafts, some injuries and retirements, you didn't have the players any more. You're still the same coach, but now you don't have a job. And it had little to do with how many 18-hour days you put in."

Sonny sat there with a stunned look on his face.

"Listen, I am more than grateful for the opportunities you gave me. I got my master's for free and got to coach in the Sugar Bowl to boot. But I also know that I wasn't really happy there, and, not to sound too cruel, I didn't want to turn out like you guys. I saw your marriage to Emily falling apart, I saw how you and the other coaches were obsessed with winning, how it came before your families and even yourselves. I saw how we had to kiss the butts of all the high school recruits. Just too many compromises, too many things I didn't enjoy doing."

Then suddenly, silence. Both realized that Craig was raising his voice. Both men realized that things left unsaid years earlier were being said, and this wasn't the time or place. After all these years, too much, too soon.

Craig quickly changed the subject. "Hey, let me tell you about the tight end. His dad is in jail for too many DWIs, his mom died in a motorcycle wreck when he was still small. For a while his grandmother raised him, but she died a couple of years ago."

"A real all-American outfit," Sonny said.

"Yeah, we're lucky we got him. We were forced to play him as a freshman, but we thought it was the only year we would have him because of all the trouble he was getting into. He figured he'd never be eligible again. But he scored the winning touchdown on the last play of a game and got mobbed by the whole team. On Monday he was the hero of the whole school, instead of the son of the town drunk. That little taste of success started him on the road to some good things."

"Does he work here?"

"Sorta. He comes in a couple nights a week and does the pots and they let him eat here a couple times a week. Brandon or one of the other guys usually comes and helps. It's a two man job."

"Where does he live?"

"At the motel you're staying at. We gave them a deal on the back cover of the sports program in exchange for giving Rob a room. He cuts some grass for them, shovels some snow in the winter. The two or three times a year they fill up the whole place, he comes and crashes on my couch for the weekend. And that ain't half the story. I'll fill you in on the rest later."

"But why doesn't he ever smile?"

"I'll tell you later."

Craig changed the subject again. "Have you seen Emily?"

"Not yet. Probably tomorrow."

"She really has done a great job with the kids. You should be very grateful."

"She's a natural. It's a breeze for her. Always has been."

"I don't know about it being a breeze. Emily once asked me to stay at her house with the kids while she went to an English teachers' convention in Columbus. The two longest days of my life. Even though Emily left detailed instructions for any possible scenario, as well as enough food for a month, I blew my first experience as a 'parent.' I was totally unprepared for Gina waking up with a temperature of 104; a toilet backing up and leaving two inches of yuck on the floor; and picking up Jill thirty minutes late for Brownies and all of her tears because she thought I had forgotten about her. I don't know much about being a parent, but I do know it isn't a breeze."

Chapter Four
Wednesday

Craig often got the credit for Rob Steele's successes, as if football and a caring coach were responsible for the kid who went from the streets to All-State. Well, it was just not true and Craig would be the first to admit it. His first experiences with Rob were not good, Craig wanted nothing to do with him. If it wasn't for the persistence of Emily Johnson, Rob Steele would not have even finished high school, let alone emerged as the school's best athlete.

As a freshman, Rob was a complete loner who didn't even have any friends to talk to at school. He never smiled. It was known to all that he was a pretty good athlete and a very tough kid. But he was undisciplined, unreliable, and had trouble with basic human skills like bathing. And everyone knew his home life was a mess.

He was the first freshman the coaches had ever moved up to the varsity, but it wasn't solely because he was so talented. They did it to keep an eye on him, and so that he wouldn't be a bad influence on the other freshmen. The coaches honestly thought it would be the only year Rob would be eligible or still in school, so why not get something out of him? They figured by the next year he would either be ineligible, in juvenile home, or thrown in that mess called foster care.

That first football season with Rob tried everyone's patience. He missed practices, cut school, didn't keep his practice stuff clean, and did not socialize with any of the other kids on the team. He kept hanging around the kids he always did from the east side of town, many of whom were older and most of whom would never graduate.

The second week of school a nonathlete upperclassman made fun of Rob because he wore the same thing to school three days in a row. Being the streetwise kid he was, Rob even got the other kid to throw the first punch. But after that it was over quite quickly, and Rob really did a number on him. Since he was the instigator, the other kid got the same punishment as Rob: three days out. But it was Rob's second major offense of the school year, and there was a chance he would be suspended.

Word got around school the next day that Rob was finished with the football team. After all the other things Craig had to watch out for, he now had to worry about Rob beating up kids in the hallways.

Emily went to see Craig in his classroom the afternoon of the fight, before he headed to practice. She had the most serious look on her face. "Craig, you and I go back a long way, and I don't think I have a closer friend on the whole faculty."

Craig just nodded his head, surprised by her sincerity.

"You have to do me one favor, and you can't say no."

"What? You know I'd do anything for you."

"You can't kick Rob Steele off the football team."

Craig was stunned. Why was she so concerned about him?

"I don't have the time to tell you why now. But tonight I'll tell you and show you. Be ready to go around eight."

At that time Craig had been living in town for several years, but that night Emily took him to a part he had never seen before. First she stopped at a convenience store and bought a carton of Winstons and a bottle of Old Grand Dad. Craig was confused; Emily hadn't smoked in years, and he knew she wasn't a bourbon drinker.

They went over the river, past the old boarded-up furniture factories, and over the tracks to the most depressing trailer park Craig had ever seen. Each trailer had more than a touch of rust, and each no longer sat exactly right on its foundation, each tilting in a different direction. If a tornado ever rolled through town, this place would be history.

Emily parked near one of the last units, grabbed the bag with the cigarettes and bourbon and said, "I haven't been back here in years."

Emily knew where she was going as she went up to the side door, pounded on it, and said, "Gretchen, are you in there? Are you home?"

From inside they heard a smoker's cough and then, "Come in, whoever you are."

They walked in on an old woman sitting in the dark, chain smoking and watching TV. She leaned over, turned on the lamp that set on the table next to her, and looked up with the saddest eyes Craig had ever seen. They came to life a little when she recognized Emily. "Emily, dear, I heard you were back in town." Emily walked over, leaned down, and the two women gave each other a long and sincere hug.

Craig looked around at the inside of the trailer: dirty dishes in the small sink, piles of old magazines and dirty clothes, dust and ash everywhere. A trash can in the corner with empty booze bottles and fried chicken carry out-buckets. One of those picture frames with circle and squares on it to place photographs hung on the wall. The pictures, which all looked at least twenty-five years old, featured an attractive teen-age girl with brown shaggy hair and a great smile. In one of the pictures she was standing next to a sixteen-year-old Emily Johnson, their arms around each other and both of them laughing.

"Gretchen, this is Craig Collier, Rob's football coach."

The old woman reached out with a limp hand and said, "Nice to meet you, young man."

Then there was an awkward moment of silence and Craig noticed the eyes of both women starting to water.

"Craig, do you mind leaving Gretchen and I alone for awhile?"

"No problem," he said, and went and sat in the car.

An hour later Emily came back out. Craig could tell that she had been drinking, she had been smoking, and she had been crying. She handed him the keys and they headed back to Craig's place in silence. Emily didn't say anything the whole way home; she just looked out the window and tried very hard to hold back her tears.

She finally opened up when they were sitting at her kitchen table and drinking coffee. "She doesn't have much time left, and she has no control over Rob," she started. "She says he's not a bad kid, but with no dad or mom, or older brother or sister, there's no guidance, no parental figure."

"Where's the dad?"

"Who knows?"

Where's the mom?"

"Dead."

"How do you fit in?"

She paused and gathered her thoughts and emotions. "Gretchen's daughter, Rob's mom, was Janice Taylor. She was my best friend in high school." Tears and emotions burst out of her like a rainstorm. "I was one of the lucky ones. I got to go away to school. I got to go off and join a sorority, and go to dances and make new friends, and have the time of my life. I even got to meet a handsome young football coach. Janice stayed behind and got a job at the factory, working in the office with her mom. And while I was out seeing the world, she started to see an older guy she met in one of the bars in town. Janice fell hard for him, and he seemed okay. But no one knew until it was too late that he had a drinking problem, and sometimes he would slap her around."

She sipped her coffee and continued. "Why she married him I'll never know. And after putting up with the drinking and the other stuff, to go and have a baby with him?"

She paused again. "I wanted to come home and have a big talk with her. But I kept putting it off. I was too busy being pregnant with Gina, picking out wallpaper and furniture for our new house."

Emily got up, grabbed the coffee pot to refill their cups and continued. "Five years later, she finally decided to leave. She took Rob to her mom's, and went back to the house to get the rest of their things. What happened next has never been too clear. The neighbors say her husband came home and beat the crap out of her, but somehow she made it to her car and drove away. He followed in his truck. The police said she was going close to eighty when she hit the bridge piling head on."

"Did he get charged with anything?"

"What? She was too mangled for anyone to see what he had done to her. The lawyers found something wrong with the neighbors' testimonies, and she had traces of pot and booze in her blood stream."

They sat in silence again for a moment. Then she said, "Rob lived with his dad for a few years. Then one day he dropped Rob off at Gretchen's and left town for good. Imagine how bad those years were."

"What's Gretchen's story?"

"She wasn't always like that. Her husband left her too, but at least she had Janice. She was her whole life. And at one time that was a nice trailer in a nice park, and a lot of kids from school lived there. And Janice was the best of the bunch. Everyone loved her. When she died it broke Gretchen's heart beyond repair. She always blamed herself for letting her daughter make the same mistakes she did."

Football players chew on their mouthpieces, it's just a subconscious habit most of them pick up. When Rob returned to practice from his suspension from school for fighting, Craig noticed his mouthpiece had a faint red tint to it, he assumed caused by blood. The next day he yanked Rob out of his gym class and took him to see Dr. McMichael, Missy's dad, one of the dentists in town.

Rob spent almost an hour in the chair while Craig read old magazines in the waiting room. Finally they both emerged and Dr. McMichael said, "Rob, wait here while Coach and I have a talk."

He led Craig into his office, shut the door and said, "I don't think the kid has ever been to a dentist. What a mess!" and he went on and explained the sad state of Rob's teeth.

"We can get him cleaned up, it's just going to take awhile. You got to make sure he makes his appointments here to see me for the next few months. I want to see him once a week. I went through with him how to brush and floss properly, and gave him a kit with some stuff in it. But that's only half the problem. The kid needs braces badly." And he explained some more about the structural problems with Rob's teeth, most of which Craig did not understand. "I know the kid has no insurance. That's no problem for the first stuff. I'll do that for free. But to do the braces right it's going to cost thousands of dollars."

They both sat there in silence for a moment, and then a slight grin came across Dr. McMichael's face.

"You guys just got a new dental plan on your insurance. A real good one. Use it yet?"

"No."

"Good, because it looks like you need braces."

Craig looked at him with confusion, remembering the sacrifices his mother made to get him braces way back in seventh grade. Then it hit him, and he too had a grin across his face that soon turned into a laugh that both men shared.

The next Friday night, when Rob was eligible to play again, he caught a touchdown pass with no time left on the clock to break a tie and win the homecoming game. It was a deep seam route where he got a step behind the safety. The ball was slightly underthrown and they both went up for it at the same time. Rob wrestled it away from the other kid, came down running and was untouched for thirty yards as he ran into the end zone and won the game. It was the type of play only big time players make. The bench mobbed him, and many of the kids in the stands jumped the fence and got into the celebration. The next morning the front page of the town's newspaper ran a picture of Rob running alone into the end zone holding the ball above him. Monday morning in school he was the toast of the town. He no longer was the kid who never smiled, or the son of the town drunk, but the kid who won his school the homecoming game.

When Craig got back to the coach's office to change for practice on Wednesday, Sonny was already there with the game tapes he had borrowed the day before and a legal pad full of notes.

"Thought I'd get down a few things that might help…" Sonny said as he left to go meet Wysocki early on the practice field.

Craig stood there for a second, staring down at the pages of notes and diagrams Sonny had left him. Then he walked over to the trash can and filed it all away.

"What are you doing?" one of his assistants yelled across the room. The rest of them stood there speechless. "The guy has coached everywhere, he might know a few things."

Craig sat down to put on his shoes and replied, "And by the end of the week he'll be telling the band what songs to play at halftime. I'm not going to get started with him. It will never end. Helping us with Wysocki is enough. Now let's go to practice."

But before Craig went out the door, he did reach in the trash for the legal pad, and threw it on the desk so he'd have some reading material that evening. Practice went smoothly, and Sonny spent most of his time focused on Wysocki and his preparation for the game.

Sometimes Emily thought of Jill as a walking time bomb. Stashed away inside of her head was everything her older siblings had gotten away with, as well as everything they got caught doing. Out of the three kids she was the only one that didn't really remember Sonny and Emily married. She really only remembered being raised by Emily.

But that didn't mean she had forgotten her father. No one enjoyed the summer trips to California more than her, and she was the one who watched every game televised in their area. And she constantly reminded all of her friends at school who her dad was.

Jill was different than Gina and Brandon. She had always known her father for what he was now. A lot of kids at school just lived with their mother, so it seemed like no big deal.

For Jill, Sonny was the guy who took her and her siblings on a great California vacation each year, including days at the beach and trips to Disneyland. He was also the guy who called her on her birthday and Christmas morning to make sure she had gotten all the presents he sent. And he was also the guy she could see on the TV most Sundays in the fall, roaming the sidelines from New England to Seattle.

But Jill was careful not to bring up her father, especially their divorce, in front of her mom; it only made her sad.

The stress in the house could be cut with a knife, as everyone waited anxiously for Sonny to arrive to take Jill to the "Father and Daughter Sixth Grade Dance." Everyone except Brandon, of course. Knowing what a big deal the women in his family made out of things like dances, he had the sense to stay away, playing video games at Johnny Adams' house.

Gina spent every moment since they had gotten home upstairs with her little sister, making sure everything was perfect. The dress their mom had bought Jill the day before fit perfectly. She looked like quite the young lady in it. Gina even let her sister wear a pair of her shoes, which came surprisingly close to fitting. And she helped Jill with her hair, so her blonde curls fell down onto her shoulders. Lastly, Gina helped Jill apply just enough makeup to look a bit grown up, but not enough to look sleazy. Gina knew neither of her parents would approve of that.

Getting her sister all dressed up for the dance got Gina thinking about something besides what she had been thinking about all day: her impending encounter with her father. It had been over two years since she had seen him in person, almost a year since she had written him, and close to six months since their last phone conversation. *Oh, so much has happened,* Gina said to herself. *He'll look right through and see I'm not an innocent little girl anymore.*

Downstairs, Emily was taking yet another lap through the living room and front foyer, making sure nothing was out of place. She wasn't sure why she was feeling this way, stressed, with a touch of impending doom. It was only Sonny picking up Jill; what could go wrong? Five minutes of picture-taking and they'd be on their way.

Sonny hustled back to his motel room after practice, where he grabbed a shower and got dressed in a shirt, tie, and his blue blazer. After he tied his always-shiny shoes he checked himself out in the mirror. *Why am I so nervous?* he asked himself.

Considering everyone's disposition, when Sonny did finally arrive to pick up Jill things went smoothly. Emily answered the door and greeted him with an awkward hug and kiss on the cheek. Jill planned her descent down the front steps just as Sonny stepped through the door. All attention turned toward her. She looked spectacular, eleven looking like twenty-seven.

Everyone's eyes followed Jill down, step-by-step. When Jill finally reached the bottom, Sonny did a quick double take between his two daughters, Jill at the bottom of the stairs and Gina at the top. For a moment, he thought they were the same person. Emily just smiled at her youngest daughter, happy that she was so happy.

"Hi Daddy, " Jill said as Sonny wrapped his arms around her, picked her up, and kissed her on the cheek. Slowly, Gina made her way down the steps, and after Sonny was done with Jill, he gave her a hug, too.

"Hi Daddy," Gina said into his ear.

"How's my girl?" Sonny replied.

Emily and Gina took turns taking pictures on the front porch, and soon Jill and her father were off to the dance.

The dance took place in the undersized gym at the middle school. Tables were covered with paper tablecloths, crepe paper fell from the ceiling, and a DJ played a mix of rock-and-roll oldies and current songs by the popular boy bands. There was even a silver ball spinning in the middle of the dance floor. And even though it was called the Father and Daughter Sixth Grade Dance, Sonny could tell there were just as many grandfathers and uncles and older brothers as there were fathers.

Sonny and Jill had a wonderful time. Because Sonny was who he was, the other "dates" immediately made him the center of attention. Every one of them wanted to get his autograph, shake his hand, or talk a little football with the Coach.

Sonny also heard a lot of compliments about his older kids. More than one Dad told him how tough of a football player Brandon was, or how much they enjoyed Gina as a babysitter.

The only time Sonny and Jill were alone was when they were on the dance floor. Just like every other middle-aged former jock, Sonny had a pair of wheels that weren't reliable anymore, so he begged off the fast ones but enjoyed dancing to almost every ballad.

And it was while they slow-danced that Jill got Sonny caught up on the latest news on her siblings. "…And Brandon's been in love with Missy since they were in middle school but Gina says she won't give him the time of day because she goes with a college guy."

"And what about Gina?"

"Gina hasn't had a boyfriend since she got sick."

"Got sick?"

"Yeah, last year. She went to a friend's house and got sick with two boys. We had to call 9-1-1 and an ambulance came and everything. They pumped her stomach! But she's okay now."

"No kidding. Gina must have really been hurting."

"She still hurts sometimes. Gina really misses you. Dad, I'm a big girl and so is she, but sometimes she cries she misses you so much."

The night ended for Sonny and Jill with a big hug in the front foyer. "Thank you, Daddy, I had the best time," Jill said as she hung onto her father.

"I did too, sweetie, I did too," Sonny replied. "Now you get on up there and get to sleep. Remember, you still have school tomorrow. I'll see you at your brother's game on Friday."

"Okay, Daddy," Jill said with one more hug before she ran up the stairs. Halfway up, she paused and turned back to her father and said, "I can't wait until I tell Brandon and Gina how much fun we had. They're going to be so jealous!" She turned, finished the steps, and disappeared into her room.

As soon as her door closed Sonny followed her up the stairs, but headed down the other end of the hallway to the bedroom he assumed was his ex-wife's. "What happened to Gina? Why didn't I know she was sick?" He said as he barged into the room.

"Hey, did you ever hear of knocking?" Emily said in her best teacher's voice, and it stopped Sonny in his tracks. She was sitting up in bed, reading glasses perched on the end of her nose, a stack of compositions in her lap. "This is neither the time nor place to discuss this."

"I deserve to know," Sonny replied. "Last time I looked I was still her father and the guy that makes sure there's a check here on time each month."

"Yes, you're still the father, but the child support is here on time each month because the team takes it out of your paycheck and sends it to me directly. If it was left up to you I would have to call you to remind you to send it each month like it was when we first got divorced," Emily said. "And this still isn't the time or place to discuss this. I have third block off tomorrow from 11:45 to about 1:00. Why don't you pick me up in front of the school and we'll go to lunch to discuss it."

Sonny didn't know what to say, but nodded his head in agreement.

"And the next time please knock. We haven't shared a bedroom together in a long time," Emily said.

Sonny turned and left and closed the door behind him.

As he drove back to his motel, Sonny realized he enjoyed the dance more than he had expected. He enjoyed picking up Jill, all the pictures her mother took, dancing the Hokie Pokie, and even talking football with the other fathers. Sonny knew Jill got a kick out of having her friends' dads ask him for an autograph. *God, I can't believe how old she's getting!* Visions of a young Gina floated through his head.

The news that Gina had been sick the year before left him feeling hollow inside. *Was that why she had such a sad look on her face this evening, or was I just imaging that?* He remembered Gina when she was Jill's age, when she was Daddy's girl, and couldn't believe she was less than a year away from going off to college. *Where had the years gone?*

Chapter Five
Thursday

Sonny and Emily sat opposite each other in the sandwich shop down the street from the high school. They finished unwrapping their lunches, and the small talk was over.

"A year ago our daughter went through a bad period," Emily started. "She acted like she was too cool to be a teenager, and she started hanging around with an older crowd, kids already out of high school. Lots of dopers and drinkers, lots of kids who never went off to college and who work shitty jobs and just hang around." Emily talked very methodically, trying not to let too much emotion enter into her voice.

"To make a long story short, she was at a girlfriend's house one Sunday afternoon, without the parents home, and three of these losers showed up. The girls let them in. After splitting several quarts of malt liquor and a bottle of vodka, and swallowing several unidentified pills, her girlfriend went into her parents' bedroom with one of the boys."

Emily took a long pause, sipped her coffee, and paused again. Sonny sat there with an anxious "what happened next" look on his face. Emily continued.

"And then the two other boys pinned Gina down on the couch, whipped out their dicks, and persuaded her to accommodate both of them."

Sonny pounded the tabletop hard enough to bounce both of their sandwiches in the air, spill over both cups of coffee, and get the attention of everyone in the establishment. Emily, without saying a word, walked over to the counter, grabbed a pile of napkins, brought them back to the table, and cleaned up the spilled coffee. She then resumed her story, in the same low, methodical voice. She kept her head down and did not make eye contact with Sonny.

" Now listen, before I go any further, I'm going to tell you one thing and you better listen…don't be critical of me. There's a lot of shit work that goes with parenting, stuff you know nothing about. All our kids know of you are trips to Disneyland, afternoons on the beach, and that country-club-of-a-life you call training camp. I've done a good job raising our kids, a damn good job. But it hasn't always been perfect or pretty."

"Why are you telling me this now?"

Emily finally raised her head and looked Sonny in the eyes. "Because it gets worse. When Gina came home that night, she went up to the bathroom and swallowed a bottle of sleeping pills."

For a moment Sonny looked like he was going to explode. He controlled himself, however, and Emily continued.

"Luckily, Craig was here for dinner that night. I sensed something was wrong, and found her on the floor in the bathroom. While I called for the ambulance he stuck his fingers down her throat and caused her to vomit."

"Craig was there?"

"And I'm lucky he was. I don't know what I would've done without him."

There was another long moment of silence as they both picked at their lunches. Then Emily spoke again. "There's another reason we should all be grateful that Craig was there."

"Oh, what was that?"

"The newspaper pays someone that works in the emergency room to keep an eye on who comes in. That night it was a nurse that Craig knows. She never called the paper. Consequently, there wasn't a story zipping across the wire services about a daughter of a pro coach trying to kill herself."

"And why didn't you at least try to call me in San Diego?"

"For one, you weren't in San Diego. You guys were playing on Monday night in Seattle and we had no idea where you were. By the time you were back home on Tuesday she was back in school."

"Why didn't you call me then?"

"Because…"

"Because why?"

"Because we figured you didn't want to be bothered. You guys got beat pretty badly in Seattle, Joe Montgomery separated his shoulder, and you had Denver coming up on Sunday. What would you have done from 3,000 miles away? You would not have come here."

Sonny sat there simmering, but he knew she was right. "What did you do to punish her? Did you get her to a shrink?"

"Actually, we did nothing. Sonny, she's a good kid who made one big mistake. Believe me, she's never going to make that mistake again. She's learned her lesson, suffered enough. On one Sunday afternoon Gina went through her whole stupid stage. She has been the model kid since then, a good student, a good older sister to her siblings. And she never goes anywhere without first telling me. She stops into my classroom at least once each day, and she always calls, even if she's going to be five minutes late."

"What about her reputation? What do the kids at school think?"

"I don't think that much of what really happened got out. And what did, got exaggerated and distorted so much it just faded away. Plus, these kids today, with all of them raised in divorced families, parents with problems, and encounters with drugs and alcohol, no one leads the perfect life anymore. No one. You'd be proud of Gina of late. She's really getting excited about going off to school next year."

"Is she still talking about Florida State?"

"No, she isn't. She's thinking about staying close to home, in state. She's thinking about Kent, OU, or Bowling Green."

"What about the boys involved?"

Before Emily could respond, they were approached by one of the ladies who was working behind the counter. For a moment, Sonny reached for the pen in his shirt pocket, thinking he was about to be asked for an autograph.

"Mrs. Johnson, I just wanted to thank you again for helping Cindy with all that ACT paperwork. We really appreciate it."

"It was nothing, Mrs. Reynolds. I enjoy helping her. Just remember, get all that financial aid information back from your ex as soon as you can. Make sure you remind him the sooner in January he gets all his tax stuff together, the better."

"I will. I have to get back to work. Thanks again, and have a nice day," she said with a smile. Then she turned to Sonny quickly and said, "You have a nice day, too."

Sonny pulled the rental car in front of the school to drop off Emily and said, "Should I talk to Gina?"

"What do you have to say?"

Another pause.

"Listen, when she's ready, you'll be ready. Don't talk to her if you have nothing to say, or if you're not ready to listen to what she has to say. I think she wants to talk to you about it. Remember, it has been a long time since you were more a part of her life than just someone she sees on TV on Sunday afternoons."

Emily had five minutes to spare before the bell rang for the next period. She rushed to the ladies' faculty washroom, locked the door behind her, and sat down on the commode. She wanted to gather her thoughts before her next class, and she didn't want anyone to see her shaking.

Gina was never the same after her parents split. As the oldest, she took it a lot harder than her siblings. Back then she was Daddy's little girl, and Sonny played such an important role in her life. In Carolina she would get up early to have breakfast with him before he left for his eighteen-hour days, and she would often wait up to have a bowl of ice cream with him when he got home. She was on the sideline during their home games, in charge of the cord that led to Sonny's headset. She was quite the sight telling all the big football players to get off the cord and out of her way. They always knew she meant business.

Their last season in Carolina one of the local papers did an article on Sonny and Gina, and the front page of the paper had a great shot of them together on the sidelines during a game with the headline "Daddy's Little Girl Plays Big Role." Gina loved the attention she got from Sonny and everyone else being the coach's daughter.

All of that ended suddenly one spring. And like her mother, Gina put it behind her and got on with her life. She excelled in school, got involved in choir and cheerleading, and always seemed to have dozens of friends. But every so often, like when she started to smoke in ninth grade, she would do something to let the world know that all was not perfect with her.

Sonny became obsessed with Wysocki's performance that week, keeping him after practice each night. Wysocki was in awe, didn't say a thing, and listened to every word Sonny said.

It was after practice that Sonny gave Wysocki the "secret weapons," a pair of golf gloves, one for each hand. Sent from the golf pro at La Quinta Country Club, Sonny had cut the ends off all the fingers and both thumbs, leaving just a covering for Wysocki's palms and the back of each hand.

After he tried them on and saw he could still snap while wearing them, he looked at Sonny and said, "What am I going to do with these, Coach?"

"Hold."

"Isn't holding illegal?"

"It's not illegal if you don't get caught. And those gloves are the same color of their uniforms, and there ain't no ref going to see you grabbing a little shirt when it is absolutely necessary. The key is not to get greedy and do it every play. You'll know when, believe me. You'll know when."

By the end of the school day Emily had one thought rolling around in her mind, Gina and Sonny. She remembered how close they had once been, and how hard Gina took all the changes that happened to their family. Emily saw a lot of herself in her oldest child, and often wondered how she would have turned out if her father had not been around when she was in high school. Emily knew Gina and Sonny needed some time alone together.

Gina, Brandon, and Jill all came home at different times on Thursday, but all of them had a smile when they entered the kitchen and smelled their mother's fried chicken and biscuits.

"Mom, what's the occasion?" Brandon asked. "You usually only make this for special events."

"Oh, I stopped by the IGA on the way home and they had chicken on sale. I figured, what the heck."

Emily left the chicken and biscuits in two big bowls on the stove, and as her kids came home they each made themselves a big plate. Also on the stove was a plate already made up, covered with aluminum foil.

Gina was the last one home, and as she fixed her own plate asked, "Mom, who's the extra plate for?"

"It's for your father. When you are done eating I want you to take it to the motel he's staying at out by the freeway. I think he'll appreciate it. Craig has had him eating all of his meals at the diner."

Gina paused for a moment, and Emily thought she was looking for an excuse not to do it. Mother and daughter looked at each other for a moment and then Gina said, "Okay, when I'm finished I'll go."

One hour later, Gina pulled her mom's car into the parking spot outside of her father's motel room. She sat there for a moment, trying again to get the courage to get out of the car and knock on the door. It had literally been years since they had spent any time alone together. Gina had not made the trip out west with her siblings the previous summer, using the math class she took in summer school as the excuse. But that's all it was, an excuse. It was just too soon after her Sunday from hell.

Gina grabbed the plate of food her mother had given her, got out of the car, and approached the motel room. Through the door she heard her father's voice talking on his cell phone. *It must be something important,* Gina said to herself, *he's using his coach's voice.*

Sonny heard the knock on the door and got up while continuing the conversation with his agent. "Tell them I'd love to do the rest of the college season and some of the bowls, but I'd rather be in the studio than on the road. See what you can do…" he was saying as he opened the door. He was surprised by the presence of his oldest daughter.

"Listen, something just came up," he said, signaling to Gina to come in. "Do the best you can and I'll either call you back tonight or first thing in the morning." He turned off the phone, flipped it shut and placed it on the dresser. He turned toward Gina and for a moment there was an awkward moment of silence.

Gina offered him the plate of food and said, "Mom thought you'd like a home-cooked meal."

Sonny took the plate, lifted a corner of the foil covering it, and took a whiff. "Thank you, honey, that's just what the doctor ordered. It's been a long time since I had some of your mother's fried chicken, and some of her biscuits, too."

Sonny took the plate and put it on the table in the corner of the room. More awkward moments of silence followed.

"Why don't you sit down," he said, pointing to the chair that went with the small table. She sat there, and he sat on the edge of the bed.

Sonny got the small talk going. "I'm really enjoying being with your brother's team. They seem like a good group of kids."

"They're really excited about having you around. It's not every day that they get to be coached by someone who's coached in the Super Bowl and the Orange Bowl."

They made small talk back and forth, but the conversation was filled with too many holes of silence. Both of them felt very awkward.

Finally Gina said, "Dad, do you remember when we lived in Carolina?"

"Of course I do. We lived in that old farm house with the big front porch."

"Do you remember when I was little and Mom use to let me wait up for you to come home from practice?"

"Sure, that used to make my day."

"Do you remember how we used to have ice cream before I went to bed?"

"I could never forget that."

"You used to always come home to put me to bed. Do you remember?"

Sonny nodded his head, remembering the little girl he used to tuck in every night.

More silence and then Gina said, "Dad, you know that thing that happened to me that Mom told you about?"

Sonny responded with another nod, and Gina continued.

"It was bad, real bad. I used some real bad judgment..." She paused, her eyes swelling with tears. "But you know the only thing I thought about when it was all over, when I woke up in my hospital room?" They looked deep into each other's eyes, tears now swelling in both sets. "All I hoped for was that you would walk into that hospital room and hold me and tell me everything was going to be all right. Dad, I needed you there..." and as she said that she left the chair, sat down next to her father, and wrapped her arms around him and cried on his shoulder. As she cried on his shoulder, he hugged and held her like he never had before.

"I doubt you would have stopped me from doing the things I was doing, but I sure wished you were there at the end," Gina said as the tears kept coming.

"I'm sorry, honey," Sonny replied, feeling very guilty and not really knowing what else to say. "I'm really sorry."

47

Chapter Six
Friday

Craig had been around football enough to know that the guys he coached against were, for the most part, pretty good people, especially on the high school level, where most of the coaches were full-time teachers. He had spent time socially with a lot of the coaches from the area at clinics, and had coached against them in other sports. He did not, however, like the coach that week, the "legendary" J.R. Jackson.

The reasons were many. J.R. reminded Craig too much of some of the coaches he had seen in the big time, full of too much ego and self-importance. When he first started coaching against him, J.R. had the best athletes in the county at Upper Olentangy. He won the league several years in a row. But he let it be known to everyone that it was his team with "my players" and "my playbook" in "my program" that was responsible for the success.

But the last several years, the talent had not been there, and he had blamed several disappointing seasons in a row on players who didn't give their all, lousy assistant coaches who didn't want to put the time in, and referees who didn't know what they were doing. It had been everyone else's fault but his.

Craig's dislike for him went back years earlier to a coaching clinic in Cincinnati. Not knowing any better at the time, Craig took J.R. up on his offer to split a hotel room for the night. Craig ended up going out for a few beers with some friends, while J.R. had to get to bed early because he was one of the speakers at the Fellowship of Christian Athletes breakfast in the morning. Imagine Craig's surprise when he finally got around to checking out the next afternoon and found charges on the room bill for several 900 phone calls and an adult pay-per-view.

But Craig really disliked him for the fact that he had never given him any credit as a coach. Craig's teams had won the last two years, but both times J.R. told the local papers that injuries and a lucky bounce or two were the reasons. Craig was a lot more new school than old school, and J.R. was old school to a fault. J.R. still treated his players like he was General Patton or Bobby Knight, and everyone else like they were lucky to be in his charge. Craig knew that if you yelled all the time then the kids wouldn't respond unless you were always yelling. Or they would get tired of it and just ignore you. Craig's players knew that when their coach raised his voice, he meant business.

Craig also knew that the guys who took that dictator attitude into coaching missed out on something: really getting to know the kids. With more and more of them from single parent households or fragmented families, teachers and coaches got stuck doing a lot more parenting than they ever had had to do.

And there was one more reason Craig did not have a high opinion of J.R. Jackson. The man was a Sonny Johnson clone. Same hair, same style of coaching attire, same strut up and down the sidelines. His voice even sounded like Sonny's. Craig had had enough of the real Sonny Johnson years ago; this fake one just got on his nerves.

J.R. treated his assistants much like Craig was treated when he was a graduate assistant: like garbage. Long hours, much of it doing useless, repetitive busy work. When things went right, J.R. took all the credit. When they didn't, J.R. blamed his assistants and players.

Football isn't rocket science. It's still only a game, and 99% of the time the team with the best players usually wins. Craig didn't like to waste anyone's time, especially his own. J.R. thought there wasn't enough time in the day for everything that needed to be done during football season. Craig had summer practice done by one so the kids could still work; J.R. kept his kids at school until after dinnertime. J.R. had his coaches at school each Sunday morning from eight until noon watching game films and making the game plan. Craig made copies of game films for all of his assistants to watch at their leisure, and they made their game plans on Monday at school during their free periods. J.R. let his assistants know he didn't like them going out after games on Friday nights; Craig always made sure to pick up the bar tab and made sure everyone had a safe ride home at closing time.

For the last several years against Armstrong, J.R. had been his worst enemy by over-coaching. Back five years ago, when he had the studs, no matter who did what, J.R.'s teams always beat Craig's. But once the talent became even, and knowing that J.R. buried himself into a game plan and lived and died by tendencies, Craig took advantage of J.R.'s over-coaching. J.R. totally relied on whatever the computer spit out, and Craig knew it.

The bus ride from Armstrong to Upper Olentangy took around forty-five minutes, as they went from one corner of the county to another. For Sonny Johnson, it was his first time on a school bus since he was a high school student.

The bus left school just as dusk was approaching, and headed out of town on the state road that led to the interstate that would take them across the county. The players were divided into two buses, seniors and starters on one, everyone else on the other. Sonny sat with Craig and several other coaches at the front of the seniors' bus.

The trip to the game filled Sonny with images reminiscent of his high school football days, traveling by school bus to games in towns in western Pennsylvania. Looking out the window, watching the sun set over the late October Ohio landscape, he was able to make out the lights of other high school football stadiums far off on the horizon. Just as names of these Ohio towns rolled by on green signs, Sonny remembered the towns of his youth, like Cranberry, Beaver Falls, and Penn Hills.

Sonny turned around and glanced back at the faces of the kids on the bus, each one of them with their own headsets on, staring off in their own little worlds. He found Brandon in the back, staring out the window, lost in his thoughts and his music.

The game was important for both teams. Armstrong Consolidated started the season 0-3 after three tough losses to three good teams. But then some younger kids started to step up, and they were going into the game on a six-game winning streak. The three early losses shot their chance for the state playoffs, however, with all of their studs except Rob Steele coming back the next year, the future looked bright. A win would give them a 7-3 record, and a piece of the conference championship.

Upper Olentangy needed a victory to win the conference outright, and clinch a state playoff bid. A loss would drop them into at least a tie for the conference, and would shut them out of the state playoffs for the third straight year. It would also be their third straight loss to Armstrong, something that had not happened in over twenty years.

The game promised to be a classic and went as expected, with Upper O taking a 20-17 lead into the fourth quarter. Both teams traded punts, and the Armstrong offense found itself on its own twelve with a very long field in front of them, and time slipping away.

It was then that Armstrong tailback Rocky Therian caught his rhythm and put the weight of the whole team upon his shoulders. Twelve yards off right tackle on first down. Another eight on a trap on the next play. Yet another big run and Armstrong found themselves in enemy territory. All these plays had been run out of an I formation, with Brandon giving key block after key block from his fullback position.

Therian's biggest run came on a third and four on the forty-three. On a stretch play he cut back to the inside when there was nothing outside, caught a couple of good blocks, and juked his way down to the twenty-one. First and ten in four-down territory.

It was then that Craig used his F.U.J.R play to take advantage of J.R. Jackson's over-coaching. J.R. knew that on first down in four-down territory that Armstrong liked to pass. J.R. also knew that if they were in a one-back set, and that one back was Brandon, they had, so far that season, passed 100% of the time. The Armstrong Consolidated Rockets' max protection was outstanding, able to pick up any blitz the whole season long. This year's F.U.J.R play would only take one personal change to be put in motion.

When they signaled in the formation, Brandon stayed on the field and Therian jogged off. Brandon panicked slightly when the play came in as 33 Draw, waiting for Therian to jog back onto the field to replace him. Brandon had never carried the ball out of that formation the whole year.

Meanwhile, on the other side of the field, J.R. got word from his assistant upstairs that it was going to be a one-back set, with the Johnson kid and a tight end in the game. J.R. knew it was going to be a pass play with max protection. J.R. signaled in to cancel the blitz he had already called, and instead called for a 3-deep zone with man coverage on the outside receivers. Everyone would be dropping into pass coverage.

Brandon was surprised when the huddle broke and he was the back still in the game and they were going to run 33 Draw. He glanced up at the line of scrimmage and it looked pretty good, if someone could get a block on the middle linebacker, who was tight to the line faking blitzes.

When Craig saw the defense he felt pretty good, too. His only worry was whether Wysocki was going to get any kind of block on the middle linebacker.

Wysocki hunched over the ball, and was scared to death as he saw the dancing feet of the middle linebacker bounce from gap to gap. *Oh my god,* he said to himself, *he's going to blitz right past me.*

Normally on 33 Draw the center takes a step backwards after he snaps the ball to show pass. But Wysocki, so filled with fear, snapped the ball and fired directly into the middle backer, who was then head up on him faking a blitz. All Wysocki had on his mind was what Coach Johnson told him all week.

But the linebacker didn't blitz, because J.R. had called it off. He was just playing around on the line of scrimmage, and as soon as the ball was snapped he started his pass drop. He read pass all across the field, except for the center, head up on him, who fired into him full force.

Wysocki made contact just as the middle linebacker was taking his first step backwards, and he got perfect leverage on him under his shoulder pads. He grabbed onto his numbers, just as Coach Johnson had shown him, and never stopped moving his feet. He held on for dear life.

In the split second after the snap Craig saw Wysocki's block; the rest of the offensive line stepping inside and giving the defensive line the outside rush; and both outside receivers running fade routes and taking the coverage into the corners. "Oh, my…" he said to no one in particular.

Instead of staying in max protection, tight end Rob Steele first faked a quick in route. He looked back at the quarterback, and raised and waved his downfield arm to let everyone know he was open. This caused the free safety to read a short pass and to step up. After three steps Steele adjusted his route upfield, and headed directly at the safety.

On the opposite sideline, J.R. felt confident they would stop the Rockets on first down. Thirty-seven times that season they had run a shotgun formation with Brandon and a tight end in the game, and thirty-seven times it had been a pass downfield to an outside receiver, both of whom were now double-teamed. Thirty-seven times, what a tendency.

Once the ball was snapped, J.R.'s confidence lasted only a second more. That's how long it took him to see the tight end go after the safety, the block on the middle linebacker by Wysocki, and to realize Brandon was going to get the ball. J.R.'s heart felt like it had dropped to his knees.

Brandon took one lateral step as if he was going to pass block, secured the ball from quarterback Ricky Marcey, and took off like a bat out of hell. After he crossed the line of scrimmage and still had no one near him, he looked downfield and saw Wysocki's block on the middle backer, and Rob Steele just about to slam into the safety. Brandon kept pumping his legs faster and faster and did not stop until he was five yards deep in the end zone.

The play had been such a game buster that Brandon stood alone in the end zone for several moments before he was swamped by his teammates. Up in the stands, Emily first hugged Jill and then everyone around her. On the track in front of the home stands, Gina grabbed Missy and the two girls hugged and screamed into each other's ears.

Everyone on the bench went crazy too, and when Brandon came off the field after the extra point, he was again mobbed by his teammates. When he was finally free he came straight for Craig, literally jumping up into his arms and yelling, "You planned that all along, didn't you?"

Craig just smiled and said, "Great run. About time you got that elephant off your back."

Brandon then went and got a drink of water, and found Wysocki, whose eyes were filled with surprise and tears. "Great block, Wyso," Brandon said as he pounded his shoulder pad.

Wysocki looked up through his tears and said, "I know, I know..."

Greg Cielec

Brandon thought he felt someone looking at him, and he glanced over the fence to where the cheerleaders were. For a brief moment, he thought he caught Missy McMichael looking at him, and that they even made eye contact. But just as Brandon sent her a smile, she turned away from him with a blank stare on her face.

"Oh my God," Brandon suddenly said aloud, as he remembered there was one more person on the sideline to see about his touchdown. He walked to the end of the bench where his father was standing. When Sonny Johnson turned towards his son, Brandon saw an expression on his face he had never seen before. He looked genuinely happy.

"Great run, Son," Sonny said, and the two wrapped their arms around each other.

The scene in the locker room after the game was filled with the happiness and enthusiasm that only a high school team can give off after winning the big one. The fact that it was the last game of the season, and the last ever for the seniors, made the emotions that much sweeter.

After a little prodding, Craig was finally able to get everyone quiet enough to speak. "Before we go our separate ways after tonight, I just want to say a few things. You know some coaches wait until the fall sports banquet to give their big emotional end-of-the-year speech. That's when all the administrators and parents and boosters are there. They love all that grown-up crap. But not me. I just want to say a few things here tonight, because tonight's the last night we're really all together as a team. No outsiders, just us.

"People come up to our coaches all the time and compliment us on what a great football program we got. But you know what? I really don't like that when it happens. You know why? I hate the term 'program.' I hate it when coaches talk about their football programs. At school we have a reading program, a music program, a lunch program. I've heard of sales programs, dental programs, incentive programs...

"We are not a program. We are a team. And, as far as I'm concerned, there is nothing better in this world than being part of a team like ours. A team where everyone works for a common goal, a team that had many great wins like tonight. Remember, great things can get accomplished when no one cares who gets the credit." He paused. " I'd like to have all the seniors come up here."

54

A moment later Craig was surrounded by a dozen young men, each with the look of exhausted joy on his face. They all put their arms around each other, with their coach in the middle, an arm around a player on each of his sides.

"I want to thank these guys for all they have done for our team the last four years. The road will go on forever, and these guys will always be a part of it. And wherever they go, they will always take a part of our team with them. They were part of a lot of big wins, a few tough losses, and many great times." Craig paused for a moment to let things sink in.

"And the last thing I want to say, what better way for it to end for these guys, for one last time on our stage…" and right then everyone but Sonny broke into a smile because they knew what was coming next.

"Right here on our stage, for one last time as a member of this outstanding team of men, to end our season correctly, ladies and gentlemen, Bobby Schaffer, God's Own Rooster."

Describing senior defensive lineman Bobby Schaffer rooster imitation in words was humanly impossible. Just the sound was funny, but with the motions and strut Bobby had developed over the years, it was hilarious, hold your gut, laugh-out-loud hilarious. And he only saved it for special occasions, winning the school's talent show two years running.

Quickly, a path was made through the locker room as his teammates started to chant, "Schaff, Schaff, Schaff." He strutted across the floor, hands and feet gyrating in all directions, and the room filled with uncontrollable laughter.

Craig glanced at Sonny taking it all in, and he wondered when the last time was that he had seen this festive of a locker room. And they hadn't even won the Sugar Bowl or the AFC, just a piece of a high school conference championship.

Before they got on the bus, Sonny found Wysocki sitting in the corner, tears still rolling down his face, coming to grips with his coming-of-age moment. "Son," Sonny said as he shook his hand, "If I had players in San Diego with hearts like yours, I'd still be the coach."

Sonny really enjoyed the bus ride back. He sat again in the front of the starters' bus, the Ohio countryside now black through the windows that were frosty on the outside and steamy on the inside.

The boys on the team were quite festive, enjoying their victory. Most of the trip was filled by attempts at singing the only three songs they all knew all the words to: the school fight song, the school's alma mater, and, of course, "Hang on Sloopy."

Sonny listened in as Craig and the coaches were going over the big plays of the game.

"Did you see Terry's catch?"

"What about Frank's hit on #33?"

"Boy, Herbie really pounded them on the sweep."

And more than once a coach turned towards Sonny and said, "Coach, your kid played a hell of a game." And, "Coach, Brandon has done that the whole year." And, "Coach, he's just a great kid."

Sonny just sat there speechless, taking it all in.

And Sonny had never seen anything like the coaches' party later that night. On the levels that Sonny had coached there was never any closure to a season. You could win the national championship in a bowl game, and ten minutes after the game ended you would be on the phone calling recruits. The morning after the Super Bowl, you'd be at the office preparing for the draft, or on a plane going to a college all-star game. It never ended.

But on that Friday night, in Moe's Bar on Maple Street in some little town in Ohio, there was closure on the season. There were also beers, more beers, a few shots, a lot of laughs, and many new and old stories told and told again.

The football coaches' party was an annual event after the last football game, and it wasn't just for the football staff. Also in attendance were the coaches from almost every other sport in the school, a few wives and girlfriends, an ex-wife and/or a former girlfriend or two, most of the faculty, and even an administrator or two was seen having a good time.

Throw in pizza and wings, a great jukebox, and the fact that no one had to get up in the morning to coach the JV team or watch game films, and it was quite an event.

Sonny, being the new guy that week on the coaching staff, spent most of the night being the new audience for all the stories all the other guys had heard over and over, the same stories coaches tell everywhere. Stories about games that were won that should have been lost, and games that were lost and should have been won. Stories about last-minute wins and last-second losses, about old coaches, and great and not-so-great players, and cheerleaders that took your breath away.

Sometime during the course of the night on the way to the restroom, Sonny grabbed the bartender, who he was surprised to find was Moe himself, and slipped him three hundred-dollar bills off his money clip. "This is for tonight," Sonny said.

"Geez, Coach, this is enough for this years' party and next. You're too used to those California prices."

Sonny just laughed. "Well, if it pays for this year and next, you'll take care of it, won't you?"

"Anything you say, Coach."

Emily had decided, before Sonny had shown up, that Friday night was going to be hers and Dr. Graham's coming-out party. When Sonny appeared, she had initially decided to postpone it, but as the week went on she changed her mind.

Dr. Fred Graham had arrived that fall as the new school superintendent, straight from the inner city chaos of the Cleveland Public Schools, where he had been a principal. A distinguished-looking man in his early to mid fifties, he had been divorced for years and had two grown children. He was enjoying his first year as superintendent, which had brought him back to the small-town life he grew up in.

He looked a little bit like Ed Bradley, the guy on "60 Minutes," with gray hair and glasses, and a quite deliberate disposition that gave off the sense that he was a good listener.

Emily had been seeing him quietly for several weeks now. This was the first time they had been seen in public in front of friends and co-workers.

Where it was going, and how far it would go, was still up in the air. But for now, it had been nice. A couple of dinners at the few restaurants around town. A trip up to Cleveland on a Sunday afternoon to see the orchestra at Severance Hall and to do some shopping. And Emily had him over for dinner last week, to let her kids meet the guy that they had surely heard about through school gossip.

"Sonny, I want you to meet Fred Graham," Emily said as she introduced her current beau to her ex-husband. "Fred's our new superintendent of schools."

There was an awkward moment of silence, as the two men shook hands and casually sized each other up.

"Nice to meet you, Sonny. Emily and your kids have had so many good things to say about you."

Not expecting the compliment, Sonny was unsure what to say.

"Fred, let me go get us a couple of beers," Emily said as she went off towards the bar to leave the two men alone for a moment.

"Hi, Dr. Graham, thanks for coming to the game," one of the young coaches said as he walked by.

"Glad to be here. Nice win," he responded.

"Dr. Graham? What's the 'Doctor' for, education?" Sonny asked.

"No, I'm afraid not. Music and theater, if you can believe it. I'm just an old song-and-dance man. Took a teaching job years ago while I tried to be a songwriter, caught the teaching bug, and have been at it ever since."

While the coaches and their friends had their party at Moe's, the players, cheerleaders, and their friends were at the Marcey farm for a party of their own. The Marceys had been hosting a season-ending party for years. Their place was perfect for that sort of thing, a big back yard for a bonfire, an old barn for dancing and music, all set behind a big old farm house where Mr. and Mrs. Marcey kept an eye on things to make sure they didn't get out of hand.

Brandon was one of the celebrities of the evening, with everyone congratulating him on his touchdown. Wysocki was also enjoying the moment, and his performance permitted him to hang out with the junior and senior linemen. All the seniors showed up, including Rob Steele, and they enjoyed their last night of being the toasts of the town.

Brandon's heart was still pounding and he was still sweating, even ninety minutes after the game. He felt a slight chill from the night air, left the group of kids he was talking to, and went into the barn and grabbed one of the old blankets he found on a shelf. He returned outside, wrapped himself up in the blanket, and sat on one of the old logs that circled the bonfire.

It was the first moment alone Brandon had the whole day, and as he stared into the fire he thought back on his big evening. In his mind he replayed his touchdown run and how he was mobbed by his teammates afterward, the big hug he got from his father, the slight moment of eye contact from Missy McMichael, and the hugs and kisses from his mom and sisters outside the locker room after the game. Yes, it had been quite the night.

"Excuse me, Brandon."

Brandon looked up at the lovely shape of Missy McMichael, shivering in the cool autumn night.

"Excuse me, Brandon, I left my coat in my car and I'm freezing. Where did you find that blanket?"

Brandon very quickly forgot about the other blankets on the shelf in the barn and said, "If you want, you can share this one with me. It's plenty big."

Missy sat down on the old log next to Brandon, and he wrapped the blanket around both of them. His heart started to pound even harder. They made a little small talk, but Brandon was scared to death he would say the wrong thing. He did not want this moment to end too soon.

"Excuse me, Brandon, do you mind if I move a little closer? There's a bump or something underneath me."

Brandon did not say no, and they moved even closer together.

"Excuse me, Brandon," Missy said as they both slightly turned and looked at each other. Brandon wasn't sure what she was seeing, but he was looking into the beautiful brown eyes of the best-looking girl in the school.

"Your touchdown was, like, the highlight of the game. Gina and I hugged each other and screamed into each other's ears. It was so exciting!"

Brandon kept listening and looking some place deep into her eyes.

"...And to see you hug your dad like that on the sidelines, Gina got all choked up."

"I think I got hugged tonight by everyone I know, from the guys on the team to my dad to my mom and sisters."

"Almost everyone..." and with that Missy gave Brandon a big, wet kiss, wrapping her arms around him. Brandon held on for dear life, still in shock. *Did that just happen?* He was unsure of what to do next. *Don't blow this.*

"Excuse me, Brandon, do you mind if I get a bit more comfortable?" Missy shifted her body so she was almost perpendicular to Brandon, with her head leaning against his chest. Under the blanket, Brandon still had his arm around her, but this new position found his hand falling lazily across her chest. She just looked up at him and smiled. He tilted his head down and gave her another long kiss.

At the end of the evening, Fred drove Emily home, and being a gentleman, got out and walked her to the front door.

Emily unlocked the door, turned back to Fred and said, "What a night."

"Yes, you have much to be proud of," he responded. An awkward moment of silence followed. Fred looked into Emily's eyes, and she looked back into his. They both took a slight step forward, and soon found themselves kissing and holding onto each other like a couple of teenagers.

As she enjoyed the moment, many thoughts went through Emily's mind. Should I invite him in? How far is this going to go? God, does it feel good. Suddenly, she stepped back, startling Fred.

"What is it?" he said.

"Oh my God, I just realized the kids will be home any minute. What would we say if they caught us?

They both burst into laughter.

"Emily, I thank you for a wonderful evening. Let's pick it up at this point the next time."

"I'd really like that," she said as she kissed Fred once more on the cheek and walked into the house.

Brandon lay in bed that night, too excited to fall asleep. He kept replaying in his mind the two great athletic accomplishments he achieved that evening. His touchdown run late in the fourth quarter that proved to be the winning score of the game, which happened in front of all of his friends and his entire family; and unsnapping, without anyone else knowing, Missy McMichael's bra while making out with her under the blanket in front of the fire at the party. Needless to say, it had been the finest night of his life.

Chapter Seven
Saturday

Gina heard the alarm go off, her brother making way too much noise in the bathroom, and her mother calling her name from downstairs. *Why did we volunteer to work the craft fair at the library? Can't I just sleep in?* she said to herself.

"I'm coming, I'm coming," she mumbled from under the covers.

When she did get downstairs, and before she got to a glass of orange juice or a cup of coffee, she was greeted by a way-too-enthusiastic mother.

"Good morning, honey," her mother greeted her with a big smile. "French toast or pancakes?"

"French toast or pancakes? Mom, you never make breakfast on Saturdays. What happened to your 'only day to sleep in'?"

Just then her brother bounced into the room, gave her a hug and a kiss, then gave his mother a hug and a kiss. Gina had to sit through ten minutes of chatty small talk, as her brother and mother discussed everything from the weather to French toast to last night's game. Finally, she couldn't take it any more. "What the hell has gotten into you two?"

They both just smiled at her and Emily said, "Is there anything wrong with just being happy?"

61

Chapter Eight
Sometime the Next Week

Sonny stayed around for most of the next week, prior to starting his new job as a studio analysis for one of the networks for the rest of the college football season.

He and Craig had several more dinners together at the diner, and during the last one they talked about many things, including their chosen profession.

"At one time, I thought I was going to be a famous and important coach like you. Well, I found out you could still be important to people without being famous," Craig said.

"Believe me, after what I saw around here the last week, you are a lot more important in this world than I could ever be." Sonny responded. "And when I get settled in, I'll make a few calls about that tight end of yours. I'll never forget the block he threw on Brandon's touchdown run. I had guys in the pros that didn't block that well."

"Oh, yeah, that reminds me," Craig said as he reached into his pocket and pulled out an envelope. "Here, these are for you."

Sonny took the envelope, opened it, removed several papers, and started to read. The papers were copies of articles from the town's local weekly newspaper, dated the previous summer. The first article was about Marcus Wilson, age nineteen, who got mugged leaving the local bowling alley. The attack left him with a broken arm, two black eyes, and several cracked ribs. The second article was about Sam Luchini, age twenty-three, who was also assaulted as he was leaving one of the sleazy bars on the town's east side. He had been knocked unconscious, and was in a coma for two weeks. He, too, suffered multiple fractures. Both articles stated that each man had a long list of run-ins with the police in his past, including a DWI, several drunk and disorderlies, possession of illegal substances, and supplying alcohol to minors.

"Geez," said Sonny. "What a couple of losers. Sounds like they had it coming. What does this have to do with the tight end?"

Craig paused for a moment, then looked Sonny in the eyes and said, "The question is what those two guys have to do with you, or, more specifically, your oldest daughter?"

Sonny paused for moment then said, "What is it you are trying to tell me? These were the two guys involved with Gina?"

Craig sat silently.

"And that Rob Steele took care of them?"

Craig was quiet for another moment, then said, "In both situations, he watched the guys for a couple of weeks until he got them in a one-on-one situation. Neither had a chance. Everyone assumes he was responsible. The only ones who know for sure are him and me, and now you."

"Why did he do it?"

"I think to pay back your ex-wife."

"Why's that?"

"When Emily heard he was living on his own, that he had no family left, she made sure he was at their house at least once a week for dinner. And speaking of dinner, do you know where he eats Christmas dinner? Emily's. She just couldn't fathom him being alone. And every summer she organizes a birthday dinner for him, too, and most of the football players and coaches come over for a cookout. When Gina got hurt, it was his way of repaying Emily."

"He really hurt them?"

One of them didn't go back to work for three months. The other left town." Sonny sat back speechless, trying to take it all in.

On his last night in town, Sonny picked up Emily and took her a couple of exits up the freeway to one of the new chain restaurants. The night was surprisingly free of stress, the conversation very carefree. They had each survived the last week and a half. The conversation turned back to another time.

"Do you remember the week in New Orleans when we played Penn State in the Sugar Bowl?"

"God, how can I forget…I conceived Jill down there."

"And what about Miami when we played Florida State in the Orange Bowl?"

"I remember the victory party on a cruise ship that lasted three days. Imagine what would have happened if you guys had won."

A short pause followed, as they looked each other in the eyes.

"I have been quite impressed with how you got the kids covered. You've done a great job with them."

"I've been doing it for a long time. I should be at least halfway good at it."

Another moment of silence was followed by a glance into each other's eyes, followed by a slight move by Sonny to hold one of Emily's hands, and possibly give her a kiss.

Emily pulled her hand back, turned her face and said, "Don't."

"I was just…"

"You were just what?"

"I was just thinking about the time…"

"Listen, Sonny, those times are all behind us now. A lot as happened since we were married; a lot has happened since we were happily married…"

"I've been meaning to say something…"

"Don't say anything. It's way too late."

"But I just thought…"

"You just thought I'd forget about everything that happened and we would…"

"It's just I never felt like this before. Being around you and the kids this week has been great."

"All these years and you never knew what you were missing. Well, I'm sorry Sonny, but it's too late. You missed too much of the game. Sure, you'll always be their dad, but I doubt you'll ever be their parent."

They sat in silence, a look of disappointment on Sonny's face as he realized she was right.

"You're going to leave sometime soon, feeling happy all over and I'm still going to be here responsible for cooking two meals a day, doing laundry nonstop, dealing with sore throats and broken hearts, and making sure everyone gets where they are supposed to be every minute of every day. It only stops for two weeks a year. And that's when you import your mother to handle most of those responsibilities."

Sonny just sat there silently, knowing everything she said was true.

"Listen, I didn't mean to be so blunt, I was just being honest," Emily said. "Listen, it's been over between us for a long time. But it might not be over for you. Where is the weather girl?"

A look of surprise crossed Sonny's face as Emily brought up a topic he had been sure they wouldn't ever talk about. "At a station in L.A."

"How old is your son with her?"

"Almost five."

"Do you see him as much as you see our kids?"

"She lives a lot closer. I see them more often, maybe once a month."

"It's not too late for you to be a parent to that boy. And it might not be too late to be a husband to her. As I remember, you two were quite chummy," Emily said, feeling too confident to pass up that last little dig.

Epilogue
Four Months Later

The press conference was at eleven. Craig did not go up for it, but Gina, Brandon, and Jill did, as well as many of their friends. Everyone got back to see portions of it on the six o'clock SportsCenter, as well as the six o'clock news on cable from Cleveland and Columbus.

The atmosphere at Emily's house was festive. Brandon and his buddies were out back playing home run derby with a whiffle ball bat and an old tennis ball. Gina and her friends were around the kitchen table looking through prom dress catalogues. Jill sat in the living room with Fred Graham, getting a chess lesson.

When six o'clock came, everyone was around the TV in the family room. First they heard an announcer in a voice-over say, "It's not every day that a head coach goes from the AFC Title to the Mid-American Conference, but it has happened to former San Diego Coach Sonny Johnson. In a move that has surprised everyone in both the college and pro ranks, Kent State University has announced the hiring of the former NCAA and AFC Coach of the Year..."

Then the screen switched to a shot of Sonny at yet another press conference. But the look on his face was much different than the last time, and it seemed a much happier situation. Sonny stood smiling behind a podium. In the background, to Sonny's right, were Brandon, Gina, and Jill. To his left was an attractive woman in her late twenties with a cute young boy who looked around five years old.

"I had other offers to return to coaching, both on the college and professional level, but KSU offered me the best fit. I'm able to come back to the part of the country I grew up in, to be close to family and old friends. I will especially be close to my children from my first marriage. My daughter Gina will be joining me at Kent as a freshman, and I'll be able to see my son Brandon play some of his high school games on Friday nights, when we're not on the road."

He then answered a few questions. You couldn't hear the question on the TV, but you could hear his response. "I'm not here to build a football program…I'm here to build a football team. A wise coach once told me it's better to have a team than a program. This university has a lot of great programs like nursing and architecture, what we're going to have is a great team."

The screen then cut back to the anchor. "Johnson chose family over big bucks by choosing Kent and a five-year contract paying a base of $140,000. The Saints were ready to offer him a four-year deal for over a million annually to be their head coach. Johnson got right to work today signing his first recruit, 6'2" 225-pound tight end/linebacker Rob Steele out of Armstrong Consolidated High School in Ohio. In other football news the Cleveland Browns announced today…"

Everyone in the room turned their attention to Rob Steele, and they couldn't help but notice the look on his face, the smile from ear to ear. He kept on smiling, and glancing quickly around the room. His smile was now three weeks old, dating back to the day he finally got his braces off after three years.

An hour later, the house was still filled with people. Craig got up to get something to drink and watched Emily as she made her rounds. She first looked in the backyard to make sure the boys weren't beating on each other. Then she grabbed the coffee pot and refilled Fred Graham's cup, as he was in deep discussion with Jill over the chessboard. Emily then glanced at the front door, once again looking for the pizza man. She then ended up next to Craig in the kitchen. He put his arm around her, and gave her a sisterly hug and a kiss on top of her head.

"Are we going to make it through the rest of the school year?" Craig asked.

"The rest of the school year? I'll be happy if we make it to the end of the week," she replied with a smile.

The End

Greg Cielec

"The Big Game"
an excerpt from *My Cleveland Story*

(*My Cleveland Story* tells the tale of three friends from high school until around the age of thirty. Set in and around Northern Ohio, from the mid seventies until the late eighties, Mate Majowski and his friends Greg and Beth go from being teenagers to adults. This scene takes place late in the book. Mate and Greg are coaches and teachers together at a suburban Cleveland high school, and on a Friday night during Christmas break in 1986 their basketball team gets to play in the first ever nationally televised high school basketball game on ESPN.)

We stood in the corridor between the locker room and the gym along the cafeteria, and the noise from the gym was so loud that for a moment we stopped and wondered what had happened. When we turned the corner and looked into the gym and the people at the opposite side saw us in our uniforms, the place really went crazy. The screaming got so loud I almost lost it. I looked over at Mate and the hair on the back of his neck was standing up, emotion filled his face.

Our players were instructed to stand next to the production guy from ESPN, who had a headset on. He was going to tell each of our kids when to run out onto the court. I remember our kids just standing there and hearing the ESPN guy yelling into his head set, "I can't hear you...I CAN'T HEAR YOU!"

The place was totally out of control. Finally he just started sending our guys out across the floor...no one could here the PA announcer...and the noise that seemed to be as loud as it could be, increased with each player's name.

This is the first great scene on the tape of the ESPN broadcast. They introduced them first, and the tape shows a head shot of each of them and an on-screen graphic telling size and statistics.

As soon as their last starter is announced, the noise level on the tape greatly increases. They cut to a crowd scene of our cheering section, and every single kid in the stands is standing and cheering.

Then the tape cuts to the corner of the gym next to the stage where we would be entering. You hear a bit of our public address announcer before he is drowned out by the crowd. "And now ladies and gentlemen, the Pride of Cleveland, the River Boro Warriors..."

The noise level on the tape just gets louder and louder. The tape zooms in on Manny, the first of our kids to be introduced. While the camera was on him, the tape does not show all the kids running from the bleachers onto the floor to form a human tunnel leading from the gym corner all the way to our bench.

It was at this point that the noise in the gym just got too loud, and on the ESPN video you can't really hear the P.A. announcer or the ESPN guys, but it just doesn't matter because the picture on the screen tells the whole story. ESPN had a handheld camera on the floor, and the tape stays with a ground level shot of our starters coming through all their schoolmates, getting high five after high five from many of them. When they finally get to Mate you can see him coming through the same human tunnel, followed by me and the rest of the team, as the kids are chanting, "Mate, Mate, Mate..."

The gym was packed to the rafters. TV cameras were everywhere. The best fucking team in the country was on the other bench. Flash bulbs were going off everywhere.

We huddled our team in front of our bench and Mate tried to talk but the players started screaming, "We can't hear you, Coach. We can't hear you..."

Mate paused and he looked around and then the team looked around and we took it all in...the people in the stands were going berserk...the noise was deafening...the gym was on fire...we were ready to do it like it's televised.

Mate circled the team as close as they could to him and said above the noise, screaming so each kid could hear, even though they were less than a foot away, "Let's just do it fellas, let's just do it!!!"

Both teams went out for the jump ball and we noticed the crowd was getting to our opponents. They stood out there waiting for the noise to die and it just didn't. The crowd never let up. They won the jump, ran a play for a lay up, and when Reggie Robinson went up for the dunk Rich Simmons went with him. Even though he was called for the foul, Rich sent the ball halfway down Robinson's throat and the crowd loved it. Robinson was rattled, and he only made one of the free throws. We came down and walked the ball inside, then kicked it back to the wing for a jumper from fifteen.

During this whole opening sequence the crowd never stopped. Our ears on the bench were ringing and no one could hear the person sitting next to him in the whole building.

Over beers later that evening the engineer for ESPN would tell us how loud it really was. "I've been everywhere. I've done football at LSU, college hoops in every gym in the East. Never have all the dials gone past ten at one time, ever. Your gym was so loud it couldn't even register on our equipment. It was the closest we have ever had to blowing it off the boards."

Playing great defense, coming down and controlling our offense, we did what no team ever did or would ever do against Washington D.C. School of Industrial Arts. We jumped out to a 17-4 lead. Their kids had yet to adjust to the noise in the gym, and we had yet to make a mistake.

When they finally called a time out, you would have thought the game was over. But there was a reason they were so good, that they had won every game for the last two seasons, as well as the *USA Today* poll. When they came back out, they were a different team. They slowed it up, because we were converting too many of their transition mistakes into points. They took better shots and cut down on their turnovers. They tightened their defense, and next thing you knew they were back in the game.

The noise never let up. Our fans stood on their feet the whole half, and every time they made a run to get even with us, the crowd would pick it up a notch. They tied it for the first time with two minutes left in the half, and we needed to do something to get the momentum back before we headed to the locker room.

Manny had the ball at half court, threw it out to the wing and faked his backside pick. He caught their guy anticipating, was able to cut to the basket cleanly, and got the give and go pass while moving towards the basket. He went up strong, yet hung onto the ball for what at first looked like too long. Robinson came over on backside help and was ready to slap the shot away, when Manny's move caught him by surprise, and he ended up hitting more hand than ball for the foul. Anticipating the foul, Manny tossed the ball straight up instead of off the backboard, the ball hung in the air as the ref blew the foul, and then it came back down through the hoop. Nothing but net for the basket and a chance for a three point play!

Manny made the free throw. They pushed the ball up court and set up a back side ali upe pass and caught us sleeping, but they missed the wide open dunk. The ball went flying off the rim and we got the rebound on the run up court, and Williams hit a fifteen foot jumper from the wing at the buzzer to take us in the half up five and with the momentum.

At the half, the noise from the gym never stopped. They were pounding on the floor to the beat of the songs the spirit band was playing, and it never eased up. The coaches went into our office while the kids rested by their lockers. Mate was ecstatic.

"Do you believe it? What a rush!!!" He went on to describe our great plays of the half. We were so excited. We came out of our office, and we could tell the kids weren't going to rest on their first half laurels.

We made some adjustments and went over our game plan again. The door opened with the ref giving us the three minutes to get back on the floor, and the noise from the gym once again blew us away.

Mate looked at the troops before we went back out on the floor. "Remember, if this is going to be the greatest night of not only our lives but everyone in that gym, the greatest night in the history of our school, we have to play one more half better than the one we just played. Don't you ever forget, every so often you've got to do the impossible. And gentlemen, we are sixteen minutes away from doing something no one has ever been able to do, and on top of it, do it on national TV."

The moment that the game turned back in our favor for good happened at the beginning of the fourth quarter. They had once again scraped back to within a bucket, and we called a time out simply to get our kids off the court after we had let them go on a 12-2 run. A couple of fast break dunks had pushed the momentum over to them and, for a moment, took the crowd out of the game.

You could say that it was planned. It was one of those "if this, this, and this happen, then we'll do it" things. Rich and his friends in the band had rehearsed the song for several weeks. Mate came up with the idea of doing it during the game, and Dave Van Husen knew it would be great for a time out late in the game that didn't have a commercial break.

This is one of the incidents from the game that just jumps out at you on the ESPN tape. The tape shows them showing an on screen graphic detailing their 12-2 run, and how many of their baskets were dunks. You hear the noise level of the crowd, constantly loud until this moment, greatly diminish. Mate stands up, a look of great frustration on his face, and signals to Manny to call time out.

The tape shows an overhead shot of both teams going to their benches, their team giving each other high fives, ours with our heads down.

The tape doesn't show what was said or done in our huddle. After a moment for our guys to sit down, towel themselves off, and get a drink, I glanced at Mate to see if he wanted to discuss anything before we talked to the kids. I noticed he was trying to fight back a smile, and I knew he had something up his sleeve.

He walked into the huddle and turned his head towards Richie Simmons and said, "Richie, it's time to get this crowd and this team back into the game."

"Anything you say, Coach," he said as he got up, split the huddle, and headed over to the stage where our spirit band and student section were.

While this is going on, the tape shows a head shot of the ESPN announcers discussing their run. While they are talking, suddenly in the background, you hear the crowd going bonkers.

Dave Van Husen was manning the dials and switches in the ESPN truck parked out in the parking lot, and he did a great job all night, especially at this moment. The next cut on the tape, with the announcers still being heard discussing the game, is a shot of the horn section of the spirit band jumping off the stage and running to set up shop in front of our student section. All of them are wearing Hawaiian shirts, one of them is carrying a saxophone that he hands to Richie as he meets them half way across the floor.

Then you hear one of the announcers say, "It's important for the Warriors to get the crowd back in the game, and it looks like that's what they're trying to do right now."

The ESPN tape switches to another shot of all the horns in front of the crowd. You can see Richie adjusting the reed on his sax as one of the trumpet players can be seen counting down, "a one, a two, a one, two, three, four!"

Then you hear the opening blast of the great Bruce Springsteen/Clarence Clemons saxophone boogie number "Paradise by the C."

For years "Paradise by the C" was always the number the E Street Band opened the second half or the first encore of their shows with. If you have a copy of the 1985 Bruce Springsteen live box set, it is the first song on side two. If you have a bootleg tape of the '78 Cleveland Agora show, it is the first song after the intermission. Mate had turned the kids in our spirit band onto it earlier that basketball season, when they had asked him for some new rowdy tunes to play at the games.

The original Bruce and the E Street Band version, which we saw performed live at least a dozen times, did the same thing each time, it got everyone up on their feet dancing and screaming and clapping as loud as they could. It was Clarence 'the Big Man' Clemons wailing away on his horn, up against Danny Federeci's Hammond organ, while 'Mighty Max' Weinberg pounded the beat.

The River Boro High Spirit Band version had three saxes, three trumpets, and two trombones blasting away the Clarence Clemons part, while assorted bass drums and snares pounded away the beat. Although not as professionally done, but with just as much heart and soul, it had the same effect. It got everyone in the gym on their feet screaming and clapping for their team. And, whatever their coaches were telling their team on their bench, they didn't hear it. Because all of their players were watching our spirit band and our cheerleaders across the floor, blasting out the tune and dancing and screaming and getting the crowd into a frenzy.

For many of the kids at school, it was their favorite moment of the game and of the ESPN broadcast. The tape switches back and forth among some great crowd scenes, kids dancing in the aisles, some close-ups of some of the more animated fans, the cheerleaders dancing in sync with each other on the floor, and the spirit band blasting away on their horns, especially Richie in his sweat-soaked uniform. As one of the kids would say Monday morning in one of my classes, "At that moment, every high school kid in the country watching that game wished that they went to our school."

When it was time to get back to the bench for some last second instructions, Richie brought the brass section, all of the cheerleaders, and the first five rows of the student section back with him to the huddle. We all surrounded Mate as pandemonium was once again completely around us. Everyone stuck a hand into the huddle on top of his, and he screamed above the noise, "Let's go out and put this one away. Defense, one, two, three!!!"

"Defense!!!" Everyone screamed as we broke the huddle, only to hear the referee's whistle blowing us a technical for too many people on the floor.

"You got to keep your fans under control," he screamed at Mate and I and, of course, it just caused the crowd to get louder.

Their token white stud, Danny Meredith, went to the line to shoot the T's. He would finish his high school career shooting 82%. At Duke for four years, he would go on and shoot 89%. Later in the pros, he will have three seasons of shooting over 90%, leading the league two of those years, and coming in second behind Mark Price in the other. But all I know is on that night in our gym with our fans screaming their heads off, he missed both technicals. He would then try to inbound the ball to one of their wings, only to have it intercepted by Jamie McGowan, who would then hit Manny on a three quarter court pass for a lay up. The crowd went crazy, and we were up by four.

After that it was all over with. There was nothing they could do. The crowd had blown them away, and we were smelling blood. We came out and ran off another ten unanswered points, and it was never close again.

They called time out for no apparent reason with :06 left on the clock and us up 66-57. We were later told by their coaches that they called time out to remind their players that it is just as important to lose with class, as it is to win with it. It's not that they had bad kids, in fact they had a great group of kids, it was just that they had not lost in over two years, and their coaches wanted to make sure they handled it correctly, especially on national television.

We got everyone in our huddle and each of us, coaches, players, and managers, just stood there taking it all in. The spirit band was blasting away at something, but the noise in the gym was so loud we couldn't hear them. The crowd was on its feet screaming and clapping. The gym was completely packed and not a soul had left. There were security cops in front of the student section trying to keep the kids off the floor.

Finally, Mate got everyone's attention. Even though we were all in a tight huddle, we could barely hear him. He looked each of us in the eyes and screamed,   "How does it feel?"

All the kids went crazy, looking around and taking it all in. "Just remember fellas, we always win with class," was the last thing he told them.

Even if I hadn't watched the ending of the game and what followed hundreds of times since it happened, the images of what happened would be something I'd never forget.

The way it is on the ESPN video really does the moment justice. The tape shows the last seconds of the game with Williams under our basket slamming the ball hard off the floor and having it bounce to the ceiling. The kids off the bench running onto the floor and mobbing him. The kids out of the stands running onto the floor mobbing the team. The players on their team standing in disbelief and staring silently at what was going on, and not believing it.

Then it shows Mate and I going over to shake their coaches' hands. What the tape doesn't tell you is what Coach Fraser said to us. "That was as fine of a coaching job as anyone has done on us. Great job fellas." And believe me when I tell you, that meant something from someone who is a living legend. The John F-ing Wooden of high school basketball.

The next moment is on the ESPN tape. They kept the camera on Mate after we shook hands, and he turns towards the camera to look out at the total chaos going on in the middle of the floor, with our team being mobbed by their classmates coming out of the stands. He then is mobbed by a group of girls from his first period class, big busty girls who go to the vo-ed in the afternoon for cosmetology classes. They kiss and hug him, and even leave some lipstick marks on his face that you can see on the tape.

He next starts to scan the crowd behind our bench, probably trying to find his mom and Uncle Gus, and much to his surprise makes eye contact with someone far up in the stands. You can tell he is greatly surprised. It is a woman wiping away the tears she is trying to keep from running down her face. She smiles at him because she knows this moment is really special, and she is just happy to be another face in the crowd.

The ESPN tape, however, doesn't show Beth up in the stands. The camera stays on Mate. You see his eyes scanning the crowd and that something really surprising catches his eyes. He looks dumbfounded for a moment, then breaks into a very sincere smile, shrugs his shoulders slightly, and wipes a tear from his own cheek. He stands almost shocked for another moment, before that moment is interrupted by him being tackled by the guys on the basketball team.

By the time we got to the locker room, a mob scene had developed. Mini-cams from Channels 3, 5, and 8 were all at the game, and all three were busy interviewing our players in the hallway. Both Mate and I got stuck talking to reporters before we even got in the door. By the time I made it into the team room, it was filled with what seemed like every basketball or football player we had ever coached, most home from college for the holidays, congratulating their younger former teammates on a job well done.

Win or lose, Mate and I both always had a moment alone with the team in the locker room after every game, football or basketball. The Old Man always did, so we always did. By the time we got all of our guys together in the team room, and all of the guests and reporters and TV people out in the hallway, we all had enough time for the magic of the victory to sink in. There had been a lot of big ones with this group of kids, but nothing like this one.

"Fellas, I just want to tell you one thing," Mate said, still with a bit of the dumbfounded look on his face, "Enjoy this one. We have had our share of victories and wins over the years, many with you guys and many with the guys before you, but this one is special." He stumbled for a second, what would the Old Man say next? "You don't ever forget a night like this, especially when something will come along later, something you don't think you can accomplish, and just remember what we did tonight. Don't forget that we still have a date with destiny in March down in Columbus, but for now, let's enjoy this one." The kids wooped it up one more time, as we retreated to the coach's office to let them enjoy the win amongst themselves.

In the coach's office was quite a crowd, including the Old Man, Tom Haggerty, Dr. Kaniecki, the Postman, and Dave Van Husen. Mate surveyed the room and then nonchalantly said as he shut the door behind us, "Just another day at the office, fellas."

A moment later there was a knock on the door and Jamie McGowan stuck his head in. "Coach, remember, I got to make the call by ten." We both glanced at the clock on the wall that said a quarter till.

"Do you want us to leave?" I said.

He paused for a moment. "No. You guys might as well stay, as long as you keep quiet. Sometimes the connection isn't that good."

Everyone in the room quickly glanced at Mate and I as we signaled for them to be quiet. We shut the door as Jamie dialed the number he read off a wrinkled piece of scrap paper.

"Hello. May I please speak to inmate James McGowan, Sr., number 01-14?"

A long pause.

"Well, what did you think Dad, did we play great or what?" And for the first time since a little league game during the summer between fifth and sixth grade, Jamie McGowan was able to talk over one of his games with his dad, because one of the places that ESPN brought the game to was the minimum security wing of the Mansfield Reformatory.

It didn't take long for everyone in the room to catch on to what was happening, and we all tried our hardest to listen in and act like we weren't at the same time. All we heard was Jamie's end of the conversation, but we all had no trouble following it.

"Ya, I know they had some great players...We worked on that all week...I think both of those guys will make the NBA...It was so loud half the time we couldn't hear the coaches in the huddle...Ya, Mom was there and Timmy and Grandpa and Grandma...I should not have taken that shot, I just got lucky...I just made him work for every shot they took...Is it time already? Oh well...the only thing that could've made it better is if you were here in person but I guess on TV wasn't so bad...and I love you too Daddy, and miss you as much as always...It was great to talk to you...Ya, just like old times...Bye, see you a week from Sunday."

When Jamie left the coach's office to rejoin his teammates, there was not a dry eye in the room.

"All Laughs and No Tears"
an excerpt from *A Poem on a Bar Room Wall*

("All Laughs and no Tears" is a chapter in *A Poem an a Bar Room Wall*, my next novel. Jeff Smolinski as he approaches forty is having a major middle age crisis, for the first time ever he hates his chosen profession, and it's been too long of a time since he was seriously involved with anyone. He starts to have reoccurring dreams about his long deceased father, who seems to be trying to tell him something, and one of the women out of his past, Amy Thomas, who he hasn't seen in years.)

Amy first entered my life over 20 years ago during my freshman year in college on a beautiful late fall day, an Indian summer afternoon, as I walked back to my dorm after class.

I was walking across the street, minding my own business, when I looked up and saw a girl who literally took my breath away. She was walking right at me with a silly grin (or was it a smirk?) on her face, her brown hair bouncing on her shoulders, her breasts bouncing on air. I tried to act cool, smiled at her as she passed, but I couldn't tell if she noticed me.

When I got back to my room I went through the university's Look Book, which featured photos, mostly high school graduation pictures, of all the new students. Hers was definitely a high school graduation picture with the name Amy Thomas underneath it. She was wearing one of those oversized turtleneck sweaters that were popular at the time, same smile across her face and big bouncy hair.

I then looked her up in the school directory and found she lived two dorms over in McNair Hall, and that she was from someplace in Virginia, probably one of those affluent suburbs of Washington D.C. that sent dozens of kids to our school.

The directory listed dorm assignments by buildings but not by rooms, so I had to find a reason to get inside McNair. As luck would have it, I was really struggling in my German class (what I was taking German for, I had no idea), and spent most of the classtime doing some serious flirting with a girl named Katie, and she lived in McNair. She had been offering help to get me through the class, and so I decided it was a good time to take it.

Katie did not take my breath away like Amy did, but she also was a fine looking girl. After class the next morning I asked to borrow her notebook to get caught up on my vocabulary work, and said I would drop it off at her room that afternoon.

Imagine the surprised look on my face the next day when I pounded on Katie's door and Amy answered. "Hi," I said, trying once again to be cool and nonchalant.

"Hello," she responded, giving me a 'have I seen him someplace else?' look. This was followed by an awkward moment of silence as we both checked each other out. I was melting, I doubt that she was.

"Is Katie here?" I said.

"Yes, she's waiting for you…got to run," she said as she walked past me with an armful of books. I walked into the room and Katie was lying on her bed, headsets on and oblivious to the world, reading a textbook from her Intro to Botany class.

After a moment or two she sensed I was there, took her headsets off her ears (I heard the Dead jamming in the background), and she looked up at me and smiled.

"Your roommate let me in," I said.

"Oh, you met Amy."

"Well, not really, she went running out of here before we got to introduce ourselves."

"She's off to meet her boyfriend. They go to the library to study together every day at this time."

Boyfriend? I was immediately crushed. How could she have a boyfriend? I tried not to let my disappointment show. I didn't even know the girl. She could have been a reincarnation of Eva Braun as far as I knew.

So I did the next best thing I could do at the time, I had sex with her roommate. I hadn't planned on it, it wasn't premeditated. I had been flirting with her every morning Monday through Friday from 8:00 until 8:50 in my German class, but this was the first time I had ever seen her outside of class.

But it was a beautiful fall day, *Working Man's Dead* was on the stereo, it was the seventies, her roommate was gone for the afternoon, and there was a bit of sexual tension in the air. The fact that most of it, at least for me, was from her departed roommate seemed insignificant.

She looked up at me and smiled and said, "Thanks for bringing my notebook."

"Thanks for letting me borrow it."

She kept lying on her bed, but took her headset off and tilted her head up towards me and smiled again. I smiled back. Something inside of me told me to lean over and kiss her. Next thing I knew our tongues were dancing in each others' mouths. Then something inside of me told me to take off her shirt, and I remember kissing the freckles on the back of her shoulders.

It was quite the experience for me, to make love with a good looking girl in a dorm room on a Tuesday afternoon. It was the first time I had participated in any sexual act that did not take place in an automobile, in a basement surrounded by six other panting couples, or on a blanket on a chilly night in the outfield of a ball diamond.

After we did it several times we laid around naked, taking turns at picking out album sides. We shared a joint. (This was at the beginning of my very brief dope period. I wasn't very good at it, Katie loved it.) As I walked back to my dorm to meet my roommates for dinner, I doubt there was a happier guy on campus.

This started my Katie McGann period in my life, and it would last until spring. We dated (to be honest I don't think we ever really dated, we mostly just had sex) until I could not keep up with her any more. I'm not talking about in the bedroom department. Katie went full throttle, and had more addictions and bad habits than anyone I had known until then. She consumed cigarettes, coffee, downers, speed, junk food, beer, tequila, and vodka on a more than regular basis. But she never missed a class, spent every quarter on the Dean's List, lettered four years in tennis, and by the end of her years at school left behind a decent track of broken hearts. We remained friends after our dormitory afternoons finished, and I remained a confidant of hers for the rest of our time in school together.

But before it was over with I fell hard for her roommate. She had a laugh that just made me melt, and the best sense of humor I had ever encountered. She would make these witty little comments, and then laugh at her own jokes. And I swear her breasts were always softly calling out my name…Jeff…Jeff…Jeff.

At first I could never figure out what she thought of me. All that winter Katie and I kept up our afternoon meetings. When we first started them, Amy would usually be gone. But as the winter went on, more often than not she would still be hanging around when I showed up. I'd flirt with Amy for a few minutes while Katie lay on her bed with her nose buried in a book, her ever present headphones on. Maybe it was my imagination, but it seemed I was, ever so slightly, spending a little bit more time with Amy each afternoon. I would be so wound up after spending a little time with Amy, that once she did leave I would just attack Katie. Often we would go at it without saying a word and with out her removing her head sets. I would later tease her about banging her while she banged her head to Blue Oyster Cult.

Spring time brought new opportunities for Katie and I and we went our separate ways. We became good friends because Katie was the only person who new my deepest, darkest secret, that I was in love with her roommate.

But there was one major obstacle that never went away, her roommate was in love with someone else. And, what mattered worse, Brad Eberly was a great guy. A class ahead of us, a member of one of the more popular frats, he was good looking, charming, and came from money. He could hold his booze, was a good athlete, drove a Volkswagen Scirroco, and did a great imitation of Curly from the Three Stooges. And he had the best girl in the whole school as his girlfriend. I thought the guy had it all.

I knew my relationship with Katie had to end when I realized only people on qualudes should have sex with other people on qualudes, and I just didn't like them and she loved them. When I would go over to McNair and Katie's lips were protruding out like a guppie, and her eyes were slightly off center and her speech wasn't quite right, I knew she was on 'ludes. But, before I could bring it up, it was Katie who ended the relationship at the end of our last afternoon together.

"Why?" I responded.

"How else are you ever going to get involved with my roommate?"

"What are you talking about?"

"You aren't fooling me, I can see it in your eyes whenever you are around her. I can see it in both of your eyes."

"Well, you're wrong. You might see it in my eyes, but not in hers." And she just looked at me with a strange expression on her face.

After things ended between Katie and I, I rarely saw Amy. When I did she was with Brad, and it didn't help matters. She remained my ideal even though I knew I never had a chance.

I have to say a few words about my college experience as a whole, and what I realized about myself and those around me at the time, and where I came from and where I was going. I attended one of the many small liberal arts schools that appear across the Midwest. I chose my school, or they chose me, for two reasons, to play sports and financial aid. I didn't have a clue about much else, and had no idea about what I was getting into.

I had a great time and have little to regret, but I also came out of it with a bit of a chip on my shoulder. Not to sound like F. Scott Fitzgerald, but I did realize that there were two types of people in my school. There were those who came from very affluent families, mostly from the East, whose parents paid the very steep full tuition. The other type of people were those of us who lived and died on financial aid. Amy's dad just wrote a check each quarter, and I knew once I graduated I'd be writing a check monthly for ten years to pay back my loans. I'm not whining about it, it was just a fact of life. I knew that because half the school was like Amy, and the other half, like me, got grants, scholarships, and low interest loans.

But it also meant that all of us one day when it was all said and done would head back, degree in hand and forever changed, to our own little world. No Tri

Delt Young Republican future Junior Leaguer was going to be happy with a guy who was planning to take over his family's sausage, keilbasi, and lunch meat stand at the West Side Market. That was just a fact of life and I accepted it. I knew I would leave school with a few close friends, tons of stories to tell my mates back home, more pretty girls on my resume than I deserved, and no dangling strings attached to another's heart.

During our middle years at school I did not see much of Katie and Amy. We each hung in our different groups, mine down at the bar I worked, Amy with her boyfriend's frat crowd, and Katie marching to her own beat.

Whenever I saw Katie she would give me a big affectionate hug and kiss, and introduce me to her latest boyfriend. She went through boys like some people go through grocery store aisles, picking and choosing on a whim. Occasionally she would bring one down to the Joint, solely, I thought, to drink the guy under the table to end the relationship. I kept hearing a rumor that she had a hot and heavy affair going with one of the profs. I didn't know if it was true or not, but a lot of people just assumed it was.

Amy spent her first three years at college being her boyfriend's girlfriend. You saw a lot of that at college. She'd meet him after class, study with him in the evenings, attend all of his frat's dances and parties. During our middle years I don't think I ever saw her without him.

The town our college was in had a neat town square surrounded by row buildings with storefronts. One block off the main square was a street filled pretty much with bars where the college kids and the townies went to do their drinking. It was just a short walk from the dorms and the frat houses, and the competition kept the price of beer down. Most kids had a regular hangout, usually a place that would let you run a tab or cash a post-dated check.

Ours was simply called the Joint, but its real name was Rufus's. Rufus was long gone, but the place was run by his son Willie, and it was a great place. Just a long room with a bar along one wall and booths along the other. At the end it opened up a bit and there was an area that served as a lunch room, dart palace, or dance floor depending on what time of the day it was. Probably what set it apart from the other establishments was the old style pizza oven in its kitchen.

Rumor had it that Rufus had won it in a card game years before. I wasn't sure if that is true, but for a dive college bar Rufus's had great pizza.

I was in the Joint almost everyday, either working or drinking or eating lunch. I felt at home there, and the mixture of school kids and town folks that hung there treated me right.

Amy never hung out there, at least never until our senior year. That was probably the most unique thing about the college crowd at Rufus's. It had always been, for some unexplained reason, a seniors' bar. Most kids latched onto a place because of what sorority or fraternity they pledged, or what sports they played. The art kids hung out at Muldoon's over by their studio, and the radio and TV crowd hung out at a place on the square. But by the time most kids were seniors they usually hung out at Rufus's. I think the crowds at the other places started to seem a bit young, and by your senior year you realized all that fraternity and sorority stuff was mostly bullshit.

Their crowd started to come in a little in the fall, and by winter they were semi-regulars. After not being around her much, and then seeing her several times a week, it appeared to me that not being someone's full time boyfriend agreed with Amy. Brad was off trying to make his mark on Wall Street, and Amy was another senior having a good time waiting for graduation.

If she came in with her crowd and I was working, she got my attention. I had given up any hope of ever getting to know her better, and I had heard rumors that plans were already being made for her wedding.

It was close to the end of the school year, maybe four weeks until graduation, on a slow Monday night when I looked up and saw Amy sitting by herself at the end of the bar. She had just been in on the preceding Saturday, but she had been with Brad who was out for the weekend visiting. I remember them both being there on Saturday because I always noticed her when she came in. I also thought she seemed a little upset with him because he spent more time hanging with some old frat brothers than with her. But they left together hand-in-hand, and I was as jealous of him as ever.

"The lovely Miss Amy, how are you this fine evening?" I said, trying once again to act witty and charming.

She smiled at me and I immediately melted.

"How is you roommate the sexual Olympian?"

"Still expanding her horizons," she said. "I'm suppose to meet her down here. Have you seen her?"

"Haven't seen her yet."

"She disappeared yesterday and today. Rumor has it her favorite professor is back in town."

We were interrupted by one of the other bartenders telling me I had a phone call.

"I'll be back…" I said with a smile as I went to answer the phone located at the other end of the bar.

"Hello."

"Don't look at her, but is my roommate there?" I heard Katie on the other end of the line.

"Yes."

"I'm not coming down there to meet her," she said in a mischievous tone.

"Do you want me to tell her that?"

"No, you idiot."

"Katie, I have no idea what you are talking about."

"Her boyfriend left today, I'm not meeting her, and she has nothing else planned for the evening. She's all yours."

"What are you talking about?"

"Here's your last chance. And Jeffrey…"

"What?"

"Don't blow it."

I strolled down the bar picking up a few empties along the way. I reached the end and looked at her again and smiled.

"Was that one of your girlfriends?" she said with a smile.

"No, just a buddy looking for someone."

"Oh."

"Hey, listen, we're kind of slow tonight and I can punch out if I wish. Mind if I hang with you guys for awhile?"

"No, that would be great. And I know Katie would love to spend some time with you."

A few minutes later I sat down next to her and for the next three hours I was in heaven. I remember telling her about the stand at the market and all the different characters that hung out there. I remember her telling me that if Reagan got elected there was a good shot her dad would get a cabinet post. I mostly just remember staring into her eyes and laughing at her laugh as she recapped some of her roommate's sexual adventures. Neither of us ever noticed that Katie never showed up.

Closing time soon came and it only seemed natural to walk her home. When we stepped outside we were surprised that the spring temperature had dropped and that there was a strong chill in the air.

I offered her my flimsy jacket but she declined. "This should keep me warm," she said as she slid her arm around me.

I wanted the walk back to her place to last forever, but before we knew it we were in front of the house that she and Katie were now sharing on Summer Street. God, did she feel right, and I don't think either of us said a word the whole way.

We stood in front of the house for a moment of awkward silence, then she turned towards me. Keeping her arm around me, she took her other and wrapped it around my neck. "Boy, was that a nice walk," she said with a smile.

Before I had time to think, I kissed her. I didn't know what to expect, and I was very surprised when the kiss just lasted and lasted and lasted.

When it finally did end she said to me, "Wow, I guess after that I should at least invite you in for awhile."

And once we got inside, and slightly before we got to the point of no return, she stopped what we were doing and looked me in the eye and said, "One thing before we go any farther. We have to agree this is just a one time thing. All laughs and no tears, okay?"

What could I say? If one night was all that I got, then so be it.

Looking back on it now from twenty years later, it was the first time for real, at least for me, that I felt love enter the sexual equation. It had its own speed and rhythm and touch. It never broke, and we stayed a part of each other.

Up until that point in my life I was never one of those sleep over guys. After the deed was done, I usually left. Call me a pig if you want, but I never felt comfortable sharing a bed with someone else. When I was in a strange bed, I'd roll around a lot. Also, a lot of the girls at school were like Katie and smoked way too much. There are not too many things worse smelling than when you wake up in the morning with your nose buried in the hair of a girl who's a heavy smoker.

But I could have stayed in Amy's bed forever. After we had gone the distance several times, and had fallen in and out of sleep, it was the time that I usually found a reason to leave. We were each lying on our sides facing one another, with our arms wrapped around one another, staring into each other's eyes.

"That was enjoyable to say the least," she said with a great smile.

I returned her smile. "You know, this is usually the moment I make some excuse about having to leave."

"Go ahead, leave when you want," she said without moving, with her eyes still fixed onto mine.

"Oh, maybe I could stay a little longer…" and I was kissing her again and our hands were everywhere and we started all over again.

When I did leave in the morning it was after I awoke curled up next to her after the best night of sleep I had ever had.

The next three weeks were a blur, and I remember that I spent every night at her house. Most nights I either worked at the Joint, or Amy and I occupied a pair of barstools usually surrounded by a group of classmates, drinking ourselves to graduation. We seemed to ignore the fact she had a wedding to someone else planned for the not-so-distant future, and the topic of her boyfriend was never brought up.

Everything and everyone around us was in constant motion, and all of our friends seemed to be cramming in as much fun as possible in the little time left. Friends who had graduated before had always come back to warn us that it was over before you knew it, and that harsh reality was now upon us.

At first we tried to be discreet about what we were doing, but when it got to the point where we were inseparable it became a hard-to-hide situation. I don't know if word ever got back to her friend on Wall Street, it was something we just ignored. But as graduation got closer and closer, reality started to show its ugly head inside of me. That big, ugly secret I knew was the truth would soon have to be confronted.

We were naked together on her bed in the second floor bedroom of their house on Summer Street. It was the day that both of us had ignored as being inevitable. She lay alongside of me, her face buried in the nape of my neck, tears crawling down both of our faces. Whatever we were feeling, it was not something we anticipated four weeks ago.

Her boyfriend was flying in that afternoon, and she had to be ready for him. At least she wouldn't have to leave soon to go pick him up at the airport, he decided to get a rental car.

"I never have felt like this before. I don't know what to do," she said.

"Hey, remember what you said our first night, all laughs and no tears," I said.

"Yeah, good thing we stuck to that," she said as the flood gates opened wider.

She was looking to me to make the final decision. I had a quote floating through my head I think I first read in a Travis McGee novel that went something like this, *when you had to make an emotional decision, the hardest thing to do is the right thing to do*. So I did it.

"Listen," I said, rolling over slightly so we both faced each other. "We got to end this today. There's no way around it."

"I still don't see why."

"We are not meant to end up together, no matter how much we care for each other. We are of different worlds you and me, and we were lucky enough to be thrown together for the last few weeks. But our backgrounds are just too different, and where you are going and where I am going might as well be two different planets."

She cried and cried and cried. I got up and sat up on the edge of the bed, facing away from her. She sat up behind me and put her arms around me, and I felt her tear filled face against my back between my shoulders.

"Amy, listen to me, what's your mother do for a job?"

"My mother has never worked a day in her life. Her full time job is trying to run everyone else's lives," she said with a slight laugh.

"Well, my mom gets up four mornings a week at four in the morning to make sausage. Do you see yourself doing that?"

"Not with my nails."

"And what do your sisters' husbands do?"

"They all work for my dad."

"I could never work for your dad. Nothing against him, but I have to go back and help my uncle and mom."

We stayed to the last possible moment, few words said, before she got up and dressed and went and met her boyfriend, and I went down and worked my last shift ever at the Joint. I knew two things to be true, that we were right to end the relationship, and I would never forget the taste of her tears upon her breasts.

That night at the Joint we were packed, as family and friends were starting to arrive for graduation weekend. My family wasn't coming down until Sunday morning, and I had planned to spend the rest of the week drunk.

I worked in a fog that last night. I was glad the Joint was busy, because it kept my mind off the events in my love life. And, I was really glad that Amy and Brad did not show up as I thought they would, seeing them together would have crushed me.

I was feeling pretty sorry for myself. I knew Amy would marry Brad and they would live in some big house in Connecticut or Long Island and he'd end up some big wheeler dealer on Wall Street. They would have several beautiful but spoiled kids named Biff and Buffy, and Brad would one day take over his dad's brokerage house and her dad would be the Secretary of the Interior and I'd get a fancy Christmas card every year with a picture of all of them around the tree. And everyone would say what beautiful kids they are and how perfect Amy and Brad were for each other.

At the end of the night Katie came in alone. She sat at the end of the bar and she was the last person I served on the last night I worked at the Joint. I walked over to her and said, "What would you like?"

She looked up at me and she was a mess. Her eyes were all red, her face puffy.

"What happened to you?"

"Just give me two double shots of Cuervo, one for you and one for me." I poured the shots, shook everyone's hand on both sides of the bar, and punched out for the last time.

We did the shot without saying anything, and I signaled for refills. I was feeling bad, but for some reason Katie was feeling worse. I waited for her to say what was on her mind. After several shots, she started to talk.

"Well, my friend, we end it as we started it, alone together," she said trying to smile. "I guess our relationships both ended today."

I wondered for a moment what she was talking about, then I remembered Amy's comment about her favorite professor being back in town.

I didn't say anything, sensing she wanted to spill her guts about things. We had another round, and then she started again.

"You know all that stuff about me and Pachinski, the English prof? Well, most of it was bullshit. I had a little fling with him two years ago, but that was it. And it was a mistake. The guy's an asshole, no matter how cool he tries to act. I can't believe I fell for his bullshit."

"I don't understand. So why did you let people think it was still going on? I know I heard Amy tease you about it several times the last few weeks."

"I needed her and everyone else to think it was going on."

"Why?"

She paused, and turned slightly on her bar stool and faced me more directly. "Jeff, do you remember the night I called you to tell you I wasn't coming down here to meet Amy?"

"Yes."

"I called you from a hotel room out by the airport. And do you know where I spent the last several days?"

"Where?"

"A room in the same hotel."

She stared at me like that information was going to enlighten me about the situation.

"I don't get it, Katie."

"Jeff, who was coming or going both times? Think for a second."

I was stumped, and then it hit me like a sledgehammer. "Brad?"

"Brad," she replied.

"Wait a minute. You mean to tell me you were shacked up with Brad the perfect boyfriend?"

She nodded her head yes.

"How long has this been going on?"

"Almost the whole time we've been here. And now it's over," she said trying to hold back a tear or two.

"You mean that your secret boyfriend, the secret boyfriend both me and your roommate and all your friends have been giving you shit about, at least for the last year, is Amy's Brad?"

I sat there and did not know whether to laugh or cry, so I handled it like I handled all my problems at that time and I turned towards the bartender and ordered another round of shots.

This book is dedicated to the memory of Chris Kowalczyk